HONORS FOR APRIL HENRY

Edgar Award Finalist

Anthony Award Winner

ALA Best Books for Young Adults

ALA Quick Picks for Young Adults

Barnes & Noble Top Teen Pick

Maryland Black-Eyed Susan Book Award Winner

Missouri Truman Readers Award Winner

Texas Library Association Tayshas Selection

New York Charlotte Award Winner

Oregon Spirit Book Award Winner

One Book for Nebraska Teens

Golden Sower Honor Book

South Dakota YA Reading Program Winner

Oregon Book Award Winner

RUN, HIDE, FIGHT BACK

OTHER MYSTERIES BY APRIL HENRY

Girl, Stolen
The Night She Disappeared
The Girl Who Was Supposed to Die

The Girl I Used to Be
Count All Her Bones
The Lonely Dead

THE POINT LAST SEEN SERIES
The Body in the Woods
Blood Will Tell

APRIL HENRY

RUN, HIDE, FIGHT BACK

Christy Ottaviano Books
HENRY HOLT AND COMPANY
NEW YORK

Henry Holt and Company, *Publishers since 1866*
Henry Holt® is a registered trademark of Macmillan Publishing Group, LLC
120 Broadway, New York, New York 10271 • fiercereads.com

ISBN 978-1-62779-589-0
Library of Congress Control Number 2019932419

Our books may be purchased in bulk for promotional, educational, or business
use. Please contact your local bookseller or the Macmillan Corporate and
Premium Sales Department at (800) 221-7945 ext. 5442 or by email at
MacmillanSpecialMarkets@macmillan.com.

First edition, 2019 / Design by April Ward
Printed in the United States of America

1 3 5 7 9 10 8 6 4 2

For my father, Hank Henry (1923–2003)
A principled and honorable man who also made
a point of telling us "I love you" every day

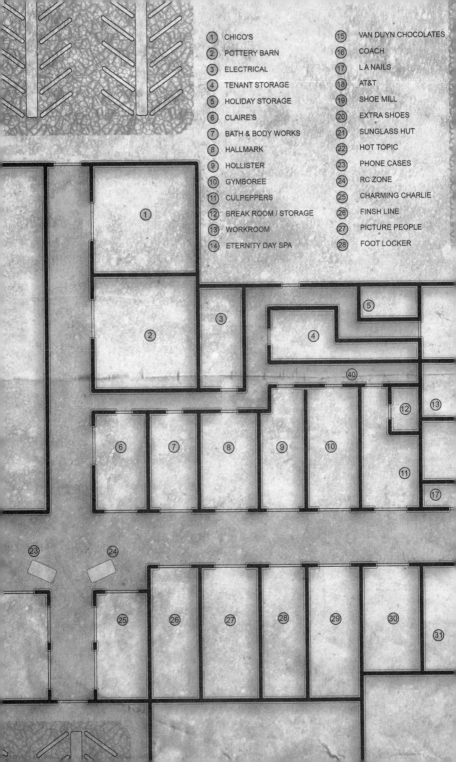

1. CHICO'S
2. POTTERY BARN
3. ELECTRICAL
4. TENANT STORAGE
5. HOLIDAY STORAGE
6. CLAIRE'S
7. BATH & BODY WORKS
8. HALLMARK
9. HOLLISTER
10. GYMBOREE
11. CULPEPPERS
12. BREAK ROOM / STORAGE
13. WORKROOM
14. ETERNITY DAY SPA

15. VAN DUYN CHOCOLATES
16. COACH
17. LA NAILS
18. AT&T
19. SHOE MILL
20. EXTRA SHOES
21. SUNGLASS HUT
22. HOT TOPIC
23. PHONE CASES
24. RC ZONE
25. CHARMING CHARLIE
26. FINSH LINE
27. PICTURE PEOPLE
28. FOOT LOCKER

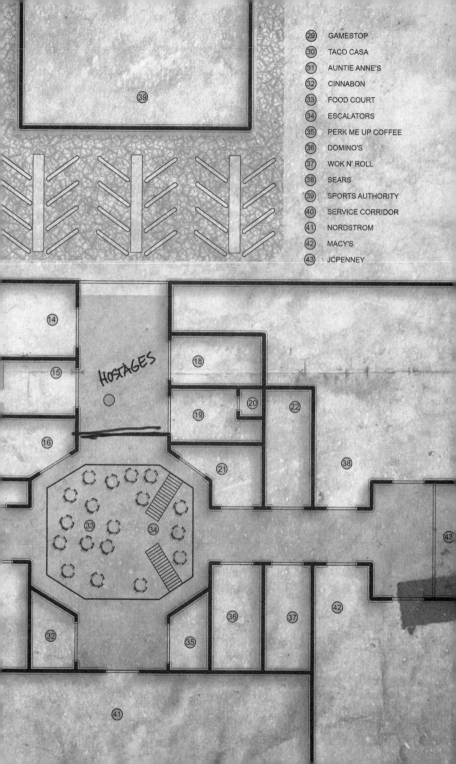

29 GAMESTOP
30 TACO CASA
31 AUNTIE ANNE'S
32 CINNABON
33 FOOD COURT
34 ESCALATORS
35 PERK ME UP COFFEE
36 DOMINO'S
37 WOK N' ROLL
38 SEARS
39 SPORTS AUTHORITY
40 SERVICE CORRIDOR
41 NORDSTROM
42 MACY'S
43 JCPENNEY

HOSTAGES

RUN, HIDE, FIGHT BACK

Within moments of Saturday's shooting at the Melbourne Square mall, dozens of officers from surrounding agencies pulled into the parking lot, helping shoppers and locking down the commercial structure while specially trained SWAT team members prepared to do a search inside. . . .

Brevard Sheriff Wayne Ivey said that training and experience from other agencies shows that in such cases, citizens who find themselves confined in a building or an area with a shooter, like the dozens of shoppers and workers in the mall when the shooting happened, often have three options.

"They can run, hide or fight," said Ivey.

—*Florida Today*, January 18, 2015

Even if the attacker has a gun and you do not have a weapon, the situation is not hopeless. There have been many active shooter incidents where people on the scene were able to subdue the attacker and save their own lives. We teach civilians to swarm the shooter and use other tactics, such as positioning themselves near the door but out of sight, so they can try to take the gun away from the shooter as soon as he enters.

The effectiveness of these principles was demonstrated in our analysis of the Virginia Tech active shooter event of 2007. In that incident, the shooter attacked or attempted to attack five classrooms. The people in each classroom responded in different ways. In the room that was attacked first and where no defensive actions were taken, 92 percent of the people were shot. In another room, where students had time to push a large desk against the door and hold it there, the shooter fired through the door, but no one was shot.

—Professor Pete Blair, Texas State University, from *The Police Response to Active Shooter Incidents*, published by the Police Executive Research Forum, March 2014

═══════════════════════════════

If your enemy is secure at all points, be prepared for him. If he is in superior strength, evade him. If your opponent is temperamental, seek to irritate him. Pretend to be weak, that he may grow arrogant. If he is taking his ease, give him no rest. If his forces are united, separate them. Attack him where he is unprepared, appear where you are not expected.

—Sun Tzu (fifth century B.C. Chinese general, military strategist, and philosopher), *The Art of War*

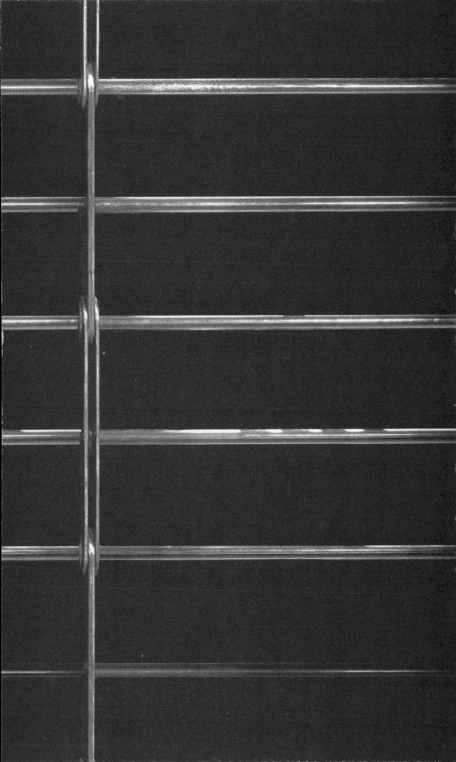

SURVIVE

WHEN THE SHOOTING BEGINS, among the dozens of people near Fairgate Mall's food court are six teenagers: Miranda Nash, Cole Bond, Javier Ramirez, Parker Gray, Amina Abdi, and Grace Busby.

The only thing they have in common is that they all want to live. But not all of them will survive.

ONE HUNDRED MILES

ONE HUNDRED MILES FROM PORTLAND'S Fairview Mall, a tractor-trailer is traveling west on Interstate 84. The eighteen-wheeler is plain, white, and unmarked. Anonymous.

It's safer that way. Safer for the three armed guards sitting on the truck's bench seat. Safer for the trailer's contents, which are rows of black buckets, filled with metal bars. Each metal bar is about the size of an ice-cube tray.

Some of the buckets hold silver bars. And some hold gold.

A single bucket of gold weighs eighty-six pounds and is worth $1.6 million.

Karl McKinley has been thinking about those buckets for years.

Once a month, this tractor-trailer makes the trip from Martin's Metals in Boise, Idaho, to a processing plant in Vancouver, Washington. The plant serves jewelry makers from Portland to Seattle.

A few days before it left, Karl paid a worker at Martin's

Metals to add a couple of extra features to the eighteen-wheeler. Features the guards know nothing about.

The first is a GPS tracker stuck to the underside of the chassis with a magnet. The tracker means that Karl can follow the tractor-trailer virtually, without arousing the suspicion of the guards.

The second addition has been placed under the dash, in the footwell. It's a device normally used to deter burglars in million-dollar homes. When triggered by remote control, it will fill the truck's cab with pepper spray.

SO MANY AND SO FAST

"THERE!" THE CLINIQUE SALESWOMAN smiles at Miranda Nash as she turns the mirror toward her. "Those colors really make your eyes pop. It's a perfect look for holiday parties."

Miranda's eyelids are covered with silver shadow, thickly edged with forest-green liner. She looks like an alien. A beautiful, big-eyed alien, but still.

"You don't think it's too much?" Ignoring the pulsing pain in her temples, Miranda tilts her head. In the mirror, the pale girl with the dark hair and eyes does the same.

"It's a statement look, but it suits you."

The saleswoman reminds Miranda of her mom. Older, but still pretty, and holding on to her prettiness with both hands, fingernails dug in. The saleswoman had sized her up when she approached the counter. Miranda watched the other woman's eyes go from Miranda's expensive shoes to the logo on her designer purse. She's probably hoping to sell her the primer, shadow, liner, and mascara, and some skin-care products.

"Can I see that foundation?" Miranda has been watching where everything came from, and she picks the item that is located farthest away. The one that will make the saleswoman turn her back.

The drawer next to Miranda's knee holds slender boxes of mascara. As soon as the saleswoman turns away, she leans down and opens it, ignoring how the action makes her head ache even more. She reaches in, grabs a half-dozen tubes, and slips them into the Ace bandage around her waist. It's covered by her oversize red sweater, the one designed to slide off one shoulder. The whole thing takes five seconds.

Miranda's made a mental map of where most of the security cameras are in this mall. The nearest one sees only her back. She's been careful not to turn her face toward it. With luck, they won't even notice that anything has been stolen until they take inventory. She knows not to leave empty packages behind. Better to take the whole thing and leave them wondering, than leave an empty box and no doubt.

To throw the saleswoman off the scent, Miranda spends an extra five minutes pretending to weigh the pros and cons of the various products. "I'm going to have to think about it," she finally tells the saleswoman. "I want to see how it looks by the end of the night."

A flash of irritation is quickly masked by a professional smile that doesn't quite reach the saleswoman's eyes. "Of course."

She's probably thinking that Miranda just wanted a free makeover so she could attend some party. And that if she even comes back to buy anything, all the products will be credited to some other salesclerk. That she has just wasted a half hour.

Guilt pinches Miranda. But she has to do this. She has to.

Because she's sick and getting sicker.

And it's still an hour until she is supposed to meet Matthew. How can she take the edge off? Maybe coffee will help. Down the mall's main hall is a Perk Me Up.

"I'll have a sixteen-ounce latte," she says to the barista. "With two extra shots."

The woman makes a face. "That's a total of four shots."

She should try living in Miranda's head. Someone's in there with a hammer. "Yeah, I know. But that's what I want."

As the woman fires up the espresso machine, which is decorated with tinsel and fake holly, Miranda leans against a pillar. Fifty feet away, she recognizes Parker's bright blond curls. Her stomach does a twist. After what happened a few weeks ago, she doesn't want to have to talk to him. To see the look in his eyes. Luckily, he has his back to her. He's with a couple of other guys from the wrestling team. They're getting up from a table, making no attempt to clean the mess of half-eaten food they're leaving behind.

Theatrically, Parker raises a napkin over his head, gives it a little shake, and then lets it fall to the floor. His audience is not only his buddies but a brown-skinned guy in a green apron. Parker's friends laugh. The busboy just looks down at the floor and grips his cart. Miranda sees his jaw clench. In case Parker turns around, she moves to the other side of the pillar and leans against it, ignoring how the Ace bandage digs into her waist.

The move puts her closer to the bell ringer from Salvation Army, who is standing next to a red kettle bearing a slogan that reads like a bumper sticker: TOGETHER, WE CAN MAKE A DIFFERENCE. The old woman would certainly make a difference if she would just stop her incessant *ding, ding, ding*ing. The noise pings around inside Miranda's aching head.

At a table about twenty feet away, a mother and daughter are both eating apples. It's weird to see such healthy food when everyone around them is consuming stuff that's deep fried, covered with melted cheese, or both.

The two look like twins separated by twenty-five years: both with dark eyes and long brown hair parted in the middle. The girl's hair is held back with a white headband, while her mother's hangs loose. They're even dressed alike, in jeans and button-down shirts. Miranda squints. The girl's right hip has a long pale logo below the waistband as well as an embroidered white tab on the back pocket. Even though she's too far away to read the logo, Miranda knows what it says: Stella McCartney. If you're going to pay five hundred dollars for a pair of jeans, you want to make sure everyone knows it.

They lean toward each other, both of them smiling, trading words back and forth, gesturing with their long-fingered hands. What would it be like to be that close to your mom, Miranda wonders. And would she like it?

Since they're dressed so similarly, she wonders if they wear each other's clothes, and if so, how the girl feels about that. At home, Miranda has learned to hide anything she really likes, which annoys her mom. Not that you can tell by her expression. She's had so much Botox that her face can't get angry anymore. She can barely raise her eyebrows. Her happiest moments are when a stranger asks if she's Miranda's sister.

The rich girl's mom is lifting her apple for another bite when a bright-red splotch about the size of a fist appears on her chest.

Miranda blinks. The red spot is growing, like a magic trick she doesn't understand. Then she registers the sounds, nearly lost in the white noise of Christmas music and a hundred conversations.

POP, POP, POP.

A man in a blue plaid shirt two tables over clutches his arm. A skinny old woman falls, her walker and her Jamba Juice cup flying out in front of her.

The sounds are gunshots. So many and so fast, she can't count them.

Miranda looks back at the girl's mom. She's tilting. Her eyes are wide and blood is bubbling between her lips. And Miranda realizes that's what's on the woman's chest.

Blood.

START TO DIE

WHEN THE BOY WITH THE MOP OF blond curls made a show of dropping his napkin to the floor, Javier Ramirez kept his face impassive. The kid clearly thought he was a real badass.

Like a piece of garbage and maybe a muttered slur were going to ruin Javier's day.

Like he doesn't have real things to worry him.

What if, despite how hard he worked this term, his grades are bad? What if the mall figures out the Social Security number he gave them is fake? What if, after Christmas, they cut his hours?

Javier is bending over to pick up the napkin when the first shot comes from behind him. Behind and above. It catches a forty-ish woman in the chest.

He recognizes the sound immediately.

Javier is already running as more people in the food court start to die.

FISH IN A BARREL

3:53 P.M.

THE SHOTS CONTINUE.

Miranda's mind is filled with a jumble of panicked thoughts. Her body is frozen as she tries to take it all in. People falling. Some are hurt. Some dead. Dozens running. Tripping over chairs in panic. Screaming. Shouting. Stampeding away as quickly as they can.

The rich girl pushes back her chair so fast, it falls over. She runs around the table to her mom, tries to catch her as she slides off her seat. The older woman's chest is now covered with blood, red and shiny as freshly spilled paint.

Is she dead? Miranda can't believe it, despite how boneless the woman now looks.

The barista drops her paper cup—just lets it splash on the floor—and flees into the back of the coffee shop. Where's Miranda supposed to go? What's she supposed to do?

Is she going to get shot? Is she going to die?

She tries to climb over the high counter. But the front

is a rounded glass display case for pastries and cookies. Her feet can't find purchase. She slides back down to the floor.

POP, POP, POP.

A bullet shatters the glass of the display case next to her chest.

Before the next one finds her, Miranda darts away.

She and the other people in the food court are fish in a barrel, the way her dad likes to say, to note how easy something is. *Like shooting fish in a barrel.*

Miranda feels for those poor fish now, swimming in frantic circles with no way to escape.

BECAUSE OF
THE BLOOD

3:54 P.M.

GRACE BUSBY TRIES TO LIFT HER MOM, but it's like trying to pick up a rag doll that weighs a hundred and thirty pounds. Grabbing her mom's wrists instead, Grace starts to drag her away. She curls her shoulders and tucks her head, hoping to provide less of a target.

She won't think about how pulling her mom over the linoleum is easier than it should be. Because of the blood.

Lately, Grace has seen a lot of blood. Most of it her own, filling up test tube after test tube. The doctors made a hole in her chest, about where her mom's is, only Grace's has a plastic cap over it.

A guy in a green apron runs up to her. His name tag reads JAVIER. "You have to leave her." He pulls at one of Grace's arms. "She's dead."

"But she's my mom." The woman Grace is dragging doesn't look like her mom, though. Not with her hair dyed dark, and her skin so pale. Her eyes and her mouth are both half-open. Neither of them moving.

"You can't help her."

"I can't leave her." Past Javier's shoulder, she sees a middle-aged guy in a business suit fall to his knees. He's clutching his neck with both hands, but red pulses out between his fingers.

"Your mother would not want you to die." He grabs Grace's wrist. "Now come!"

She stumbles after him.

CAN'T BE REAL

A S SHE RUNS FROM THE COFFEE SHOP, Miranda tilts her head back. The shots are coming from the second floor of the mall, which is open in the middle. There are no stores up there, just office space, the two floors linked by escalators. Three men in black ski masks are leaning over the railing and shooting long black guns, like AKs or something.

An older man shoves his wife behind him and then catches a bullet in the chest. Miranda lets out a scream as he falls to the floor. This can't be real.

But she knows it is. And the next person shot could easily be her. She has to get out of here. Now.

In the last few months, Miranda has come to know this mall better than most of the people who work here. In addition to knowing the location of every camera, she also knows every exit. Now she ducks underneath an escalator and runs toward the hall that leads outside.

WAITING TO DIE

3:55 P.M.

AMINA ABDI WAS SPACING THE HANGERS one inch apart when she spotted it. A discarded Perk Me Up cup. Because the store sat near the food court, people seem to think they could wander in with a drink, or sometimes even food. Pinching the cup between her fingernails, she carried it to the trash. She ignored the looks Hannah and Giselle shared. Instead of working, they were leaning against the counter, gossiping.

On Amina's shifts, she never stops moving. There's always something to do, if you look. She makes sure that everything's in place, appearing exactly as it should. On the days she's scheduled, you'll never find an XS shoved in among the size Ls. She's determined to show Culpeppers that she's just as good as any other employee—if not better—even if her bosses seem uncomfortable with her hijab. That even though the manager has hinted about Culpeppers's "all-American vibe," Americans can be all kinds of things. Including Muslim.

Now there's some kind of disturbance out in the mall.

Moving to the entrance, Amina tries to make sense of it. A fire alarm starts to blare. In the food court, people are screaming, stampeding in all directions. Some lie crumpled on the floor. As she watches, an old woman topples off an escalator. Just lands on the floor and lies there, unmoving. And that sound, which she knows only from movies and cop shows—are those gunshots?

Hannah and Giselle push past Amina and start running. Careening through the food court. Then a bullet hits Hannah in the back and sends her sprawling. Amina screams, without meaning to. Giselle takes one look behind her and then sprints faster.

When the mall isn't open, Culpeppers closes with a metal roll-down security shutter. If Amina pulls it down, will it stop bullets?

She doesn't know, but it's better than nothing. It's better than standing here, waiting to die.

PANIC

T HE FIRE ALARM STARTS SHRILLING OVER-
head as Miranda runs past the Shoe Mill. The sound
partially masks the screams behind her.

Laden with bags, shoppers are coming out of the
stores. Most of them don't seem to be in any hurry. They're
acting like it's a drill, like it won't make any difference if
they ignore it. Then a man in a tan sweater barrels into
the hall. His face is pale, his mouth and eyes wide. His fingers are clamped around his biceps, where the fabric is
soaked with blood.

People look in the direction he came from, toward the
food court. Miranda risks a glance over her shoulder. It's
rapidly emptying out. In the middle of all the tables and
chairs, a woman wearing a red scarf jumps out from
behind the busboy's cart, where she had been hiding.
Screaming, she runs toward the corridor where Miranda
and the others are.

She doesn't make it.

The shoppers around Miranda begin to panic. They scream, swear, drop their packages, call out each other's names and to God.

And as Miranda pushes past them, they surge toward the exit doors.

NONE OF THEM

EIGHT MINUTES AGO, PARKER GRAY AGREED to let his little sister, Moxie, buy a pretzel by herself. He'd given her a five-dollar bill, pointed her in the direction of Auntie Anne's. She liked talking to people, and people liked talking to her. Seven years old, curly blond hair, and big blue eyes. Cute as a bug, everyone said.

Cute to everyone but Parker. She was more a weight around his neck. Today was teacher in-service training, which meant a day off from school. He should have been having fun. Instead he was a free babysitter, since his parents were both at work. But it wasn't like he was going to sit at home watching episodes of *Dora the Explorer*. He could at least hang out with his friends while Moxie alternately played with his phone or stuffed her round little cheeks with treats.

Now his friends have already sprinted away. Everyone who can still run is running. Parker stands in the middle of the food court, spinning. Screaming over the shrill of the fire alarm. "Moxie! Moxie! Moxie!" Not seeing her anywhere. Auntie Anne's is deserted. His mind plays a panicked loop. Is she hurt? Is his sister dead?

A bullet zips past his ear and buries itself into a pillar. The space has emptied out. Chairs overturned. Drinks puddled on the floor. Blood puddled on the floor. And people slumped in such awkward sprawls that he knows they must be dead.

But none of them is a little girl in a red coat.

TRAPPED

MIRANDA PUSHES THROUGH THE CROWD toward the exit doors.

She's only a dozen feet away. But something is stretched across the exits. Cable bike locks, black rubber-coated braided steel, now link together the silver handles of each pair of doors. She pushes on the nearest door anyway. It opens an inch before the cable catches it.

Through the door glass, she sees people running across the parking lot into the gathering dusk.

Miranda's trapped. She and all the people behind her. There're only two ways out of this hall. One is through the locked doors. The other is through the food court, where the shooting started. Where the few remaining people are frantically trying to leave before they die.

And any minute, one of those men will come running down the escalator and finish what they started.

VIDEO GAME

T'S LIKE A VIDEO GAME. THAT'S WHAT COLE Bond tells himself as he runs along the edge of the food court, sheltered by the overhang, past the bodies that lie crumpled on the linoleum floor.

That lady in the blouse who got shot first, she wasn't real. None of this is real. It's just an excellent animation. Maybe on one of these 3-D TV sets they have now. If he wanted, he could press the pause button. And if he turned around, his own couch would be at his back. He could get up and go to the fridge in the garage and get another beer.

He tries to tell himself that these bodies never existed outside the game. They never had real lives that got cut short. The coppery smell hanging in the air, that's just his imagination.

When Cole's feet slip in blood, it becomes harder to deny reality.

But he has to. Because if he acknowledges that all this is here and now and real, if he acknowledges what just happened with his two older brothers, then something inside Cole will break.

Ahead of him, a girl in one of those Muslim headscarves is trying to pull down Culpeppers's metal security shutter. It's not much, but it's better than nothing.

Cole can't do anything for the lifeless bodies on the floor, but maybe he can stop this surreal horror from happening to more people.

LIKE HER LIFE
DEPENDS ON IT

MIRANDA HAS TO GET OUT OF HERE. TO get to any of the other exits, she is going to have to cut back through the food court. But there're fewer and fewer people left alive out there, and those few are even more obvious targets. She ventures back to where the hall meets the food court. In front of LA Nails, sheltered by the overhang, she tries to figure out what to do. How to stay alive.

She spots Parker underneath one of the escalators. He's screaming his little sister's name as he frantically scans the area.

The busboy Parker was taunting is dragging the rich girl whose mother was shot across the open space. They are almost clear when there's another *POP, POP, POP*. He grabs his thigh and keeps lurching forward.

A whistle carries even over the fire alarm. Miranda looks for its source. A tall, thin guy standing just inside Culpeppers pulls his fingers from between his lips. On the other side of the entrance is that dark-skinned clerk, the one who wears a headscarf. She beckons Miranda with an urgent hand. With the other, she's pulling down the roll-down metal security shutter.

Miranda runs toward the closing shutter like her life depends on it.

Knowing that it does.

4:00 p.m.

DISPATCH: Police, fire, or medical?

RON SKINNER: Police! We've got people being shot here!

DISPATCH: Okay. Tell me who you are and your address.

SKINNER: Ron Skinner. I work security at Fairgate Mall. And there's people being shot here!

DISPATCH: Okay, Ron, take a deep breath. Is there still active shooting?

SKINNER: I don't know! Hurry. Please hurry. They shot Gabriel and Zach. They work here too. I'm not sure where Timmy is. All we're issued is pepper spray and zip ties. And they've got assault rifles!

DISPATCH: I'm dispatching cars now. How many shooters are there? What's their location? Another caller stated that they were in the food court.

SKINNER: There's a lot of them. I'm trying to check all the cams. They started in the food court, but now they're all over. If they figure out I'm up here in the security office, they'll kill me, too. You've got to get your people here now! Please, please. I don't want to die!

BEFORE HE SEES US

Miranda's not the only one desperately making for Culpeppers. Ahead of her, the rich girl and the injured busboy are also heading for the store and the slowly lowering metal security shutter. The top of one of his pant legs is already dark and shiny with blood. His arm is looped over the girl's shoulders. As thin as she is, she is somehow half carrying him.

How close are the men with guns? Miranda looks back over her shoulder. Parker's in the same spot underneath the escalator, spinning in frantic circles with his hands outstretched. He's stopped yelling "Moxie!" but it's clear he's still looking for his little sister. If Miranda didn't already know it was Parker, if she hadn't seen him just fifteen minutes ago, she would not recognize him now. His mouth is wide and turned down at the corners, his face streaked with tears.

When her eyes focus past Parker, Miranda freezes. On the far side of the food court, one of the killers is coming down the escalator. Instead of running down the steps, he stays on his stair as it descends, as calm as a casual shopper. A casual shopper with an automatic rifle in his hands. He's dressed all in black, including a black ski mask with holes for his eyes and mouth. He's like a bug or a monster. Or a terrorist.

Is that what they are? Terrorists?

Over his clothes, he wears something like a short black apron with narrow, deep pockets holding red rubbery bricks with wires coming out of them. After a beat, Miranda's brain supplies the term. It's a suicide vest.

The escalator is otherwise empty, but at the bottom there's a pile of three or four bodies. One of them, a woman with curly black hair, is still moving. Her legs churn weakly against the red-streaked linoleum.

Without any hurry, the man raises his rifle and fires. Her limbs jerk and then stop.

The shot breaks the spell that has held Miranda. She has to get out of here! The killer's gaze is still focused in front of him. He isn't looking her way. Not yet. But in a minute he'll turn. He will turn his head and he will see her and he will kill her.

She's just ten feet from Culpeppers. Ten feet from the metal shutter that might save her. The shutter that is already down to chest level as the busboy and the rich girl duck underneath it.

Still, Miranda turns back, ignoring the voice in her head screaming she's a fool. She sprints toward Parker and yanks his wrist, spinning him toward her. "Come on!" she says, her voice an urgent whisper that barely competes with the shrill ringing of the fire alarm. "Before he sees us."

He resists, but she tugs harder, her eyes on the gunman, who is stepping off the escalator.

Instead of following her, Parker gasps. Not in horror, but in something closer to joy. He's spotted something in the hall with the locked doors that Miranda just abandoned. He tears his wrist from her grasp and races away.

Miranda turns back toward Culpeppers. The metal roll-down shutter is almost to the floor now. All she can see are knees and feet. And one head and a beckoning arm. It's the guy who whistled, his face contorted. He's not making any sound, but Miranda can read his lips.

He's mouthing "Hurry!"

A foot from the rattling shutter, Miranda throws herself on her belly and rolls underneath.

Just before it closes.

4:01 p.m.

DISPATCH: All units, be advised, reports of active shooters inside Fairgate Mall. Possibly at the food court. 68 and 53, respond.

UNIT 68: 68 copy.

UNIT 53: 53 copy.

DISPATCH: One reporting party is a security officer on-site with access to cams. I've got ambulances en route.

UNIT 68: Confirm shooters still on scene?

DISPATCH: Affirm. First RP reports they're still inside, multiple shots fired. Second report, from the security guard, is at least eight, probably male, unknown race, black clothing, possible AR-15s.

UNIT 53: What about the other security guards?

DISPATCH: RP says they're down.

UNIT 68: Notify SWAT for call out.

DISPATCH: Affirm. SWAT's been notified.

UNIT 68: 68 on scene.

DISPATCH: Copy.

UNIT 53: 53 about two blocks away.

UNIT 68: I'm at the south side, 53. Dispatch, we're gonna need more units. There's at least five exits on this side, and there's people pouring out of them. But I'm not hearing any gunshots.

DISPATCH: Copy. All available units, respond to the Fairgate Mall.

UNIT 43: 43 on my way.

UNIT 41: 41 about ten minutes out.

UNIT 68: [shouting in the background] I've got at least three who've been shot, but there're hundreds of people just running around. We need more cars. We need to set up a perimeter.

DISPATCH: Copy. I have 43 and 41 and who else?

UNIT 45: 45 just entering the property.

UNIT 14: Unit 14 en route from the substation.

UNIT 77: 77 on the way, but traffic's congested on 26.

UNIT 115: 115 is on I-5, but it's backed up as well.

DISPATCH: Any plainclothes responding, make sure you have your raid gear on.

UNIT 53: [moans in the background] This is 53. I've got at least five more injured in the parking lot. One male with chest wound appears critical.

DISPATCH: Copy. Fire is responding.

UNIT 68: Call Tigard, Beaverton, Oregon City, Salem, Vancouver, and anyone else for additional support. We're going to need everyone we can get.

DISPATCH: Copy.

UNIT 45: I got another person outside shot, a female in the leg. We need rescue hot.

DISPATCH: 45, your location?

UNIT 45: East side of the mall on foot.

DISPATCH: Copy, 45. We'll alert rescue.

UNIT 14: [sirens in the background] 14 on-site, west side. No gunshots heard.

DISPATCH: Confirm, no gunshots heard?

UNIT 14: Affirm. Not since my arrival.

UNIT 68: 68. The shooting appears to have stopped. I'll assume command. Have fire stage in that old Sports Authority lot. It's freestanding, on north side of mall. I want at least eight units establishing a perimeter and controlling traffic. For now, command is in front of Nordstrom on south side. Nordstrom opens directly into the food court.

DISPATCH: Copy.

IT'S YOUR LUCKY DAY

4:02 P.M.

WHEN MIRANDA YANKS AT PARKER'S wrist, he doesn't have time to wonder why she's in Fairgate Mall or why she, of all people, is trying to save his life. Because Parker catches a glimpse of a small figure dressed in red.

Moxie!

Shaking off Miranda's grip, he takes off after his sister. Sticking to the perimeter, sheltered by the overhang of the second floor, he sprints flat out.

Parker darts into the corridor where he just saw the flash of red. Even though he's lost sight of her, Moxie has to be here, because there's no way out. Ahead of him, the exit doors are chained shut. Behind him is the food court, where the only people left are dead or dying, and at least one of the killers is on the hunt. Moxie must be among the couple of dozen people frantically milling around, or maybe in one of the small stores that lie on either side. With a wrestler's agility, Parker cuts through the crowd, squeezing between a woman wearing a white visor and apron and a middle-aged guy dressed head to toe in Blazers gear. Parker zigzags between a kid he vaguely recognizes from school and a girl who looks like a teenager but has a baby in a stroller. Past an old guy in high-waisted jeans and white puffy tennis shoes, a young woman in impossibly high heels, three college girls clutching shopping bags and one another. Santa is here too, or at least the guy who was posing for photos a few minutes ago. Now he sits on a bench, his face red and sweaty. Parker dodges and weaves and slips, his gaze bouncing from one person to another: from an older black lady to a forty-ish businessman to a guy with a bushy beard and gauges. To a man with a shaved head hiding behind a pillar, a gun in his hand. To a middle-aged guy holding his arm like a tourniquet, blood welling between his fingers.

But no Moxie.

She must be in one of the stores. On one side is a Shoe Mill, and an AT&T phone store. On the other is a Coach store, a Van Duyn, and something called Eternity Day Spa. They are all small enough that the only way in or out is through each store's entrance from inside the mall. Moxie must be hiding in one of them, either in fear or blissful ignorance. Waiting desperately—or maybe just with an impatient giggle—for Parker to find her. He hopes it's the second one. Hopes that she has no idea what's going on. Hopes that he can snatch her up, keep her from seeing the dead, and find a way out.

The fire alarm suddenly stops. For a second, the silence is as loud as the piercing shrill had been. Then it's filled by the sounds of people crying and freaking out and yelling into their cell phones and asking each other what to do.

Parker is about to dart into the nearest store, the Shoe Mill, when a metallic clatter makes him turn. It's one of the ski-masked killers. He's pulling a seven-foot-tall folding metal security gate across the end of the corridor, right where it opens out into the food court. His AK is slung on his back. One side of the gate is bolted to the wall. It rattles along on casters, opening like an accordion. As soon as the guy reaches the other side, they will be penned in like animals. Animals at a slaughterhouse.

The crowd's panic ratchets up even higher. The guy with the gauges starts to run toward the rapidly closing opening. But on the other side are two more guys wearing ski masks, both of them shouting, "Stay back!" and pointing their rifles at him and the people behind him.

Parker imagines bullets mowing half a dozen people down. But then the guy's shoulders slump and he steps back.

Just before the security gate is all the way across, the killer who was pulling it steps inside. His lips are as full as a girl's. In his head, Parker christens him Lips. Lips swings his rifle in a half circle so that they all step back.

All three killers are wearing suicide vests. One of the two men on the other side of the gate locks it with a padlock. He has a dark mole just underneath his left eyebrow. Mole points the rifle at the people they have penned in. The third killer puts a megaphone to his mouth. His eyes are the silvery blue of a wolf's.

"Listen up, everyone," Wolf says. "If you want to

live—and I'm supposing you do—you have to be quiet and you have to do what we say." His tone is matter-of-fact. "Because if you disobey us, you will be killed. To begin with, anyone who is still on their phone, turn it off. Now!"

Parker thinks to look for the man with the shaved head and the handgun, the one who was hiding behind a pillar, but he's disappeared. If that guy shoots one of the killers, will that trigger the explosives?

"What do you want from us?" asks a black woman with silvered dreads.

Wolf says, "First of all, none of you should be talking. And certainly not talking back." He points his rifle at her and she flinches. "I could shoot you to make my point. But I won't. Not this time. But the next person who talks, I will put you down like the dogs you are."

The only sound is the *drip-drip-drip* of blood hitting the floor from the wounded man's arm.

"As for what we want—we want the world to listen. You're here to make sure that people pay attention. And we don't need any competing messages. Which means all of you have to give me your phones. Every single one. Take them out of your pockets and purses and slide them across the floor to me. Because if we catch one of you with a phone, you'll die." Casually, he points his rifle at the group, aiming it at one person, then another. For a heart-freezing instant, it's aimed at Parker's head, but then it moves on.

One by one, people bend down and send their phones sliding along the floor until they clear the four-inch gap at the bottom of the gate. If the phones don't quite make it, people close to the gate kick them the rest of the way. Mole starts tossing the phones into an empty Macy's bag.

"November, report in," Wolf says into his mic. "November. Over."

As Wolf waits for an answer that doesn't come, Parker's fingers touch the edge of his phone, which is in his back pocket. Parker's blocked from view by a plump middle-aged woman in front of him. Instead of pulling out his phone, he slips his finger to the side and toggles it into the silent position.

After Mole is done, Wolf nods at Lips, who goes to the door of the Shoe Mill. "Anyone hiding has to come out now!" Lips yells. "If we find you later, we'll kill you."

He repeats himself at every store. A guy in his twenties wearing khakis, a pressed blue shirt, and a name tag appears in the doorway of the phone store. A sixty-ish woman in a white hairnet comes out of Van Duyn, anxiously twisting her hands. Both are made to surrender their phones. The AT&T guy has three.

But Moxie doesn't appear. Where is she? Parker never prays, but now he prays that she has somehow run very far away. That she has found an exit and is now being evacuated by the police. Because the alternative is too awful to contemplate.

Wolf comes back to the metal security gate. His posture is relaxed, his voice unhurried. "People, you may not know this, but you are at war. And like all wars, civilians sometimes get caught in the cross fire." The smile visible through the mouth hole of his ski mask does not match the cold gaze coming through the eye holes. "Sorry about that."

Everyone is silent, watching Wolf alertly. "If there is a hell, then we'll be in good company with a lot of fighter pilots who also had to bomb innocents to win the war. But you should know that you are serving a more noble purpose than simply being victims." His gaze takes them all in. "You are the key to changing everything."

Wolf points through the security gate at the kid Parker recognized. His name is Joe or Joel—something like that—and he's a year behind Parker at school. "You. In the glasses." Joe/Joel's black-framed glasses are sliding down his tearstained face. "Come here."

The kid doesn't move. Lips comes up behind him and pokes his back with the rifle.

With a whimper, the kid shuffles forward, a wet stain spreading over the crotch of his pants.

"It's your lucky day, kid." Wolf's grin is humorless. "You're going to live. We're going to open this gate and let you out." He reaches into his pocket and pulls out a fistful of flash drives. "You're going to put these in your pockets, and then you're going to run down to the end of that hall and cut through Sears and go outside with your hands in the air. You're going to give these to any reporters you see. You're the one who is going to get our message out."

JUST A SHELL

AFTER MIRANDA ROLLS UNDER THE METAL pulldown shutter, it hits the floor with a bang. Her heart leaps in her chest like a dying fish flopping on a boat deck.

Pressing her lips together, she forces her lungs to still as she strains to hear if Parker will be shot. The bike-locked hall he ran to is just around the corner, about a hundred feet away.

She hears running footsteps and muffled shouts and screams, layered over the blare of the fire alarm, on the far side of the shutter. But no shots. What is she hearing? More victims? The bad guys? Maybe even the cops?

Finally Miranda lets herself breathe again, a series of hitching gasps. She pushes herself to a sitting position. Her body feels heavy and clumsy, a sack of flesh she can barely animate.

There are four other teens in the store. On her left is the dark-skinned girl in a turquoise headscarf, the one who just lowered the metal shutter. She works here, at

Culpeppers. Her name, Miranda remembers, is Amina. Her eyes are wide enough that they are rimmed with white. "This can't be real," Amina says, more to herself than anyone else. "This can't be happening."

On her right, the guy who urged Miranda under the shutter stands with his fists clenched. His dark hair falls over his eyes, and he holds his mouth so tightly that his lips have disappeared. He's dressed in jeans and a plain black T-shirt.

The girl whose mom just died leans against the counter, head down, sobbing wordlessly, high-pitched *huh-huh-huhs*. Heard just by itself, Miranda thinks, it might almost sound like laughter.

The busboy sits on the floor, his back against the counter. His eyes are closed, his face taut with pain. He's pressing his palms on the front and back of his thigh, over the places where the bullet came and went. Miranda squints to read the name tag on his green apron. JAVIER.

Javier opens his dark eyes and looks at her. Despite his efforts, blood is already puddling on the white linoleum.

"We should try to stop that bleeding," Miranda says to no one and everyone. Grabbing two acid-yellow sweat-shirts from a stack, she scuttles forward on hands and knees.

Javier shifts his hands so she can sandwich his leg between the two sweatshirts. Then she ties the arms of the bottom sweatshirt over the top one.

"Thank you." His bloody fingers squeeze her palm. His eyes are so dark, they don't seem to have pupils.

Amina is staring at Miranda. Her eyes narrow.

"Wait—it's you!" Her tone is almost indignant. A month ago, Amina caught her walking out of the store with a foil-lined Culpeppers shopping bag filled with stolen cashmere sweaters. As a result, Miranda has been banned from the store.

People are out there dying, and this girl is still thinking about the rules. Miranda starts to laugh. She can't help it. The sound flirts with hysteria. It's too loud. What if someone out there, one of the men with guns, hears her over the fire alarm?

Putting her hand over her mouth, she tries to stifle herself. She can taste Javier's blood, metallic and salty. She wants to throw up. She wants to scream, she wants to cry. She wants to be anyplace but here.

When Miranda finally speaks, she manages to keep her voice to a half whisper. "What are you going to do, make me go back out there again?"

"No," Amina says. "Of course not." She looks away, her mouth twisting.

Miranda looks away too. The rich girl is lost in her own world. She locks her fingers in her hair as she mutters, "Oh my God, Mom, please, no, no, no. Don't be dead, Mom. You can't be dead!"

The guy who urged Miranda to roll under the shutter steps closer. "Wait—was that *your* mom who got shot first?"

The wailing pauses, and the girl's eyes flash to him. Her expression is a wordless answer.

"I am so sorry," the guy says, wincing in sympathy. His eyes are light gray. "That's awful."

The girl chokes out, "But what if she's not dead? What if she's just hurt? I should go back out there."

"Look—" Javier begins, then interrupts himself. "What's your name?"

"Grace." Her eyes dart back and forth between him and the security shutter.

"Trust me, Grace. She's dead." His voice is as flat as his words, with only a trace of an accent. "Your mama is dead."

"How can you know that?"

"She's not the first person I've seen die." He closes his eyes again.

Miranda exchanges a curious glance with the other guy. What does this Javier person know, anyway? Then she realizes that she knows something too. She swallows and says, "I'm sorry to say this, but I think Javier's right. I saw one of them come down the escalator. He was killing anyone who was still alive."

"Even if my mom is dead, I can't just leave her out there." Grace's voice is high-pitched, distorted to a quaver. "That's my mom."

"But that's *not* your mom," the pale-eyed guy says in an urgent whisper. "Not anymore. That's just—just a shell." His mouth turns down hard on the corners. "And she would want you to live."

"Who are you and what would you know about what my mom would want?"

"I'm Cole. And that's what any parent would want for their child."

"Well, Cole, you don't know what my mom would

43

want. Maybe she wouldn't want to be alone. You guys don't know anything about her. Whether she's dead, what she would want . . ." Grace stands up and takes a step toward the shutter.

Miranda grabs her wrist. "If you go back out there, you'll put all of us at risk."

"But they've stopped shooting." Grace tries to pull free, but Miranda won't let her.

"They've stopped because anyone left out there is dead."

Suddenly the fire alarm cuts off.

Miranda holds up her free hand. "Shh!"

Everyone freezes. From outside, in the direction Parker ran to, comes a series of sounds. Rattling metal. Announcements made through what sounds like a megaphone. Miranda can make out some of the words. Something about the world listening. Something about giving up their phones. And then they all flinch at a sound. It's muffled, but it sounds like a shot.

"We have to get out of here," Miranda whispers. "If they figure out we're in here, they'll kill us."

Amina points. "The metal security shutter will protect us."

Javier opens his eyes. "That don't mean anything. I've seen bullets go right through car doors."

Miranda doesn't want to know how Javier knows these terrible things. She points toward the rear of the store. "Where does that door go to?"

"To the service corridor." Amina's face lights up. "Which eventually leads to an exit." She hurries over, pushes it open, and sticks out her head. But before anyone can think about following her, she yanks it closed again. When she turns back, she's shaking so hard, her whole body trembles. "They're killing people out there, too. There's a body right there. I think it's Linda from Pottery Barn." She shakes her head in disbelief. "Linda!"

Everyone slumps as the strings of hope are cut. "Can *they* get in here from out there?" Miranda whispers.

Amina shakes her head. "Not unless they have a key for this store. And only employees have those."

So the five of them can't leave, but it's not safe to stay, either. According to Javier, bullets could stitch through the metal shutter like it was tin foil.

"Everyone, turn off the ringers on your phone." Cole slices his hand through the air. "We don't want them to hear us."

Miranda's phone is already on silent. Closing her eyes, she forces herself to stop picturing how they are going to die. Forces herself to think. Three months ago, her school did a lockdown drill. She remembers sitting in the far corner of a dark classroom while someone out in the hall rattled the locked door. It was like playing hide-and-seek, holding your breath in the gloom and trying not to giggle. Fun, not frightening. Sure, you knew bad things went down in other schools, other places. But stuff like that always happened to someone else. It would never happen to you.

What had the sheriff's deputy told them in that assembly? Now it comes back to her. To run if they could. To hide if they couldn't. To fight back if they must.

With killers at both store exits, running is out of the question. They're hiding now, but if Javier is right, sitting behind this metal roll-down shutter isn't offering them much protection.

A man's voice, just outside the shutter, makes her jump. Addressing himself to anyone hiding in the mall, he says that this is their one chance to leave. That he will let people go now and only now. And that if they stay and are found later, they will be killed. After a pause, he repeats himself, only he sounds farther away.

"Maybe we should open the shutter and go?" Grace whispers.

"No! We can't trust them." Cole's voice breaks. "They'll just kill us all."

"But if we stay here and Javier's right, that metal shutter isn't enough protection," Miranda says. "We need to get farther back from it." She points. "Where does that other door go to?" She thinks she knows, but she's not sure.

Amina follows her finger. "A storeroom."

"Let's go." Miranda gets to her feet and looks at Cole. "Help me get Javier back there."

THE WORLD'S BEST REALITY SHOW

4:07 P.M.

AFTER THE KID NAMED JOE OR JOEL RUNS off, Parker and the other thirty or so trapped shoppers stare at Wolf in silence, a silence broken only by a little boy who is crying hysterically.

"That's getting on my nerves." Lips raises his gun. "Make him stop."

His mother desperately tries to shush the boy, but he just cries harder.

A man in a pinstriped suit steps closer to the security gate. Forgetting about the crying child, Lips moves to block him, but Wolf waves a hand to indicate that it's okay.

The businessman's voice is pitched low, but Parker is close enough to hear him. "Look, man, just tell me what you want and I'll get it for you. You want money? I have nearly a thousand dollars on me, and I'll give you even more if you let me go."

Wolf tilts his head. "Money?" He lifts the megaphone and speaks into the mouthpiece. "You're offering me money?"

Parker's blood chills as Lips jabs Businessman in the ribs with his rifle. With a grunt, he steps back and raises his hands. Only now does he look uncertain.

"You think this is about money?" Wolf's voice is a lash. "You think that if you have money you get to call the shots, and the rest of the people here"—he waves his rifle so that it takes in the whole crowd—"they can just die, for all you care?"

"I'm s-s-sorry," Businessman stutters.

Wolf is just getting started. "You are what America has become. A place where money is the only thing that matters. But you're going to help this country wake up to what's really important. If they think it's acceptable to leave people dead or dying, or to abandon them in their hour of need—wait until it's broadcast right in front of their eyes. We're going to make it so they won't be able to look away. This is going to be the world's best reality show. Broadcast live." His grin is full of menace.

Wolf's gaze takes in all of them. "In less than an hour, you'll all be the lead story on CNN. Tomorrow, you'll be on the front page of every newspaper. In a few days, you'll be on the cover of *People*." He nods as if they should be pleased. "And how you behave yourself will dictate whether there's a black box around your story, or whether you can give interviews later as a survivor. If our demands are met, we will release you. Until then, you need to stay calm and not panic. No one will be hurt if you do what we say."

Parker thinks that's a lot of ifs, but he keeps his face impassive.

Wolf nods at Lips, who goes over to a janitor's cart parked next to a bench in the center of the hall. On top are two bundles of stiff white plastic cords.

"Now you're going to zip tie each other's hands in front," Wolf says. "Anyone over the age of five. One loop around each wrist, and make sure both wrists are hooked together. And if you don't do a good job, both of you will die."

A low, shifting murmur is broken by a cell phone ringing to Parker's left. It's the theme from *Rocky*.

People back away from a big man in a green down jacket who is about ten feet from the security gate. His hand frantically roots around inside one of his coat pockets as he struggles to silence his phone.

Mole and Lips swing their rifles in his direction, but instead of lifting his own AK, Wolf reaches into the back of his waistband. He pulls out a pistol with a silencer screwed onto it. Calmly, he steps to the gate and then fires a single shot to the man's chest. Despite the silencer, the sound is still a muffled clap. People stifle their cries with their hands. The man's eyes widen and he stays on his feet for several long seconds. The sound of his breathing, rapid and bubbling, fills the hall. Finally he drops to his knees and then slowly crumples until he is facedown on the floor.

Wolf's voice is as unemotional as if he had just swatted a mosquito. "Any more phones out there?"

Three more cell phones suddenly go sliding along the floor.

Businessman is the one who zip ties Parker's wrists

in front of him. He leaves a little slack. Parker can't tell if it's on purpose. Still, it doesn't seem like a good idea to try to slip out of them. Not right now. But he feels a pulse of hope.

While they work in silence punctuated by low sobs and distant sirens, Wolf walks out into the food court. It lies at the intersection of four hallways. He goes to the hall opposite theirs, the one that leads to Nordstrom, lifts his megaphone to his lips, and says, "If you're still in the mall, you can leave now and we'll let you go. But this is your only chance. If we catch you hiding later, we'll kill you."

Nordstrom's security shutter is down. It's made of thin metal slats set an inch apart, partially revealing the store's darkened, deserted depths. Most of the other stores just look empty. But then a woman in a gray dress appears in the doorway of a Sunglass Hut. She freezes at the sight of Wolf, but he simply says, "Go on. Get out of here. While you still can."

She cuts through the food court and runs down the hall to Parker's right, so fast that it's more like a controlled fall. She sprints past kiosks selling phone cases and remote-control cars, and Parker waits for Wolf or Mole to shoot her in the back. But they let her go. Others must have been watching and listening, because four more people dart out of various stores and go scrambling after her.

Wolf's not being altruistic, Parker realizes. He just doesn't want any surprises. He already has more than enough hostages penned up in the hall. Better to encourage the ones he can't control to leave than to have his head on a swivel.

At the other two intersections, the ones Parker can't see down, Wolf repeats his invitation.

And then the only people left are trapped between the bike-locked doors and the security gate.

As Wolf comes back to the gate, Mole shouts, "We need some of you to line up against the glass doors. Come on, do it now!"

As Lips begins to herd people toward the bike-locked exit doors, Parker takes one step away, then another.

"And all of you at the doors, I want you facing the parking lot," Wolf commands. "I want them to see exactly what is at stake if they don't meet our demands. I want them to see who they're going to have to kill to get in here."

"Come on, hurry up," Lips says. "Don't make me shoot someone to make you go faster. Line up shoulder to shoulder."

"Santa!" Wolf yells. "You get up in front of the doors. You'll be the next trending topic on Twitter."

The guy dressed as Santa starts moving through the knots of people. His tearstained face is nearly as red as his outfit.

As people move toward the windows or away, Wolf speaks in a lower voice into the mic on his shoulder. "Come in, November. Do you copy? November?" When there's no answer, he switches to "Romeo, have you seen November? Over."

The answer that comes from his mic is short and decisive. "Negative."

Parker is at the entrance of the Shoe Mill now. Everyone is focused on what's happening at the glass doors. He takes one more step back and into the store. Now he can't see any of the terrorists, which means they can't see him. But he can still mostly hear them.

"Kilo, the hostages are secured," Wolf says. "Repeat, hostages secured."

Kilo's voice issues from the killers' mics. "Good. How many casualties?" Since his voice is coming only from their mics, wherever Kilo is, it's not in this hall.

"Nine in the food court. Possibly more who were initially able to leave. One here. So far." Wolf's voice is filled with disdain. "He tried to keep his phone."

"The other guards?" the unseen Kilo asks. As Parker slips deeper into the recesses of the store, he wonders how far away Kilo is. How many other killers are there?

"Taken care of. And Romeo's in touch with the cops."

"Did you distribute the message?" Kilo's voice is barely audible.

"Yes," Wolf says.

"Then we wait."

Wolf starts to respond, but his words fade as Parker keeps walking backward into the shoe store.

@jennyhkoin

Portland Police confirm there has been a shooting at Fairgate Mall.

@carriefriday

NOT AGAIN. Praying for everyone at #FairgateShooting. Stay safe. 🙏

@SaraKiplinger

Until we know what happened, all I feel comfortable saying about #FairgateShooting is I'm angry—yet again.

@Portland Police

PDX FD units responding to reports of 20-victim shooting incident at Fairgate Mall. PDX PD is working to clear the scene.

@LuPodmove

Oh great. Another mass shooting. Seems like daily occurrence for whatever reason. Sickening! Thoughts with those in #FairgateShooting.

@naturalknots

#FairgateShooting hits very close to home. Its privilege to be here not a right & one we all share together. When will craziness stop?

@MsCampbell Reads

Portland shooting looks v bad. Good luck to law enforcement & God bless. Our police are so appreciated! #FairgateShooting

@tracybarrynews

Active shooter in Portland, OR. Police confirm 4–8 shooters wearing masks and possible body armor. No one in custody. Several shot.

HOW LONG

MIRANDA LEANS DOWN AND GRABS Javier's hand to help him to his feet. After a pause, Cole does the same on the other side. Once Javier is up, he loops his arms around their shoulders. He grunts when he puts weight on his right foot, his fingers clamping onto Miranda's upper arm. He smells of acrid sweat and coppery blood and a tiny bit like sweet shampoo.

Together they lurch past the cash register and the dressing rooms. In their wake is a trail of red drops. If the bad guys do get past the shutter, they will know exactly where they are.

They stagger into the storeroom. About fifteen by twenty feet, it's filled with tall black metal shelving units stacked with neatly sorted clothing. In the back, a small desk sits next to two rows of short lockers. In the corner, an open door reveals a small bathroom with a toilet and sink.

Amina closes the storeroom door behind them. Her mouth is twisted as she stares at her phone.

Miranda, Cole, and Javier make for the chair in front of the desk. Miranda picks out her own unsmiling face on a bulletin board, then looks away, hoping no one else notices.

She starts to lower Javier into the chair. But Cole's not doing the same. Instead, he uses his free arm to sweep two stacks of plaid sweaters off the nearest shelf and onto the floor.

"He needs to get his feet higher than his head or he'll go into shock." Cole's words are brusque, almost impatient. He kicks the sweaters to spread them out, then he and Miranda lower Javier as carefully as they can. Still, when Javier's back touches the floor, he grimaces and half rolls onto his side.

Miranda helps him lift his feet onto the chair. All the moving around has loosened the makeshift bandage. "I'm going to tighten this," she says, taking the ends of the sleeves. He nods and then clenches his teeth. It's like squeezing a bloody sponge. Should she try to make a tourniquet? She sees a shard of a memory: Matthew with a belt around his biceps. Miranda shakes her head, forcing herself to focus on this room, this guy whose lifeblood is hot under her palms.

"Thank you," Javier says. "Again."

She just nods and wipes her hands on her jeans, remembering too late that there's a bathroom. How long can they take cover back here until they are hiding not with a bleeding boy but with a dead body?

Taking out her phone, she sends the same text to both of her parents, knowing it will produce very different results. Her dad will spring into action. Her mom will probably fall apart.

Shooting at Fairgate Mall. Hiding in Culpeppers. Plz tell cops. Someone shot in leg.

As Miranda finishes, Amina looks up from her phone. "I have been trying and trying, but no one's answering 9-1-1. How is that even possible?"

"It's possible because everyone here who can still dial is calling 9-1-1," Cole says. "They're overwhelmed. We're on our own." His tone is no-nonsense, but his hand trembles when he pushes the hair out of his eyes.

Grace is sitting with her back against the side of the desk. She shakes her head. "No, no, no." Her voice rises, breaks. "Someone is coming to rescue us."

"I wouldn't count on it," Cole says bluntly. "Didn't you hear what the shooters said about taking hostages?" Miranda tries to remember what she heard on the other side of the metal shutter. "And if there's hostages, the police will hang back and negotiate. They won't want to come barging in, not if that risks everyone getting shot. So this could take a long time." He opens the desk's top drawer and starts rifling through it.

Grace's only answer is a whimper. She starts to rock back and forth.

"This can't be real," Amina says. "It's like a movie. Or the worst nightmare ever." She closes her eyes. "I just want to wake up."

"None of us can afford to check out, not if we want

to live." Cole opens another drawer. "Look around and see what you can use as a weapon."

But all the room holds is clothes. What are they supposed to do, blind the killers with a glitter-encrusted sweater?

After rooting around in the desk, Cole comes up with a three-hole punch and a pair of scissors. "We need to be ready to attack if they get inside the store."

Miranda doesn't want to pin her life on someone wielding a three-hole punch. "Can't we lock that door?" she asks Amina.

But the other girl just shakes her head.

Miranda gives the nearest shelving unit a tentative push. It doesn't budge. She leans on it with all her weight. It shifts the tiniest amount, maybe a quarter of an inch. Still, it's something.

"If we can use one of these shelves to barricade the door, they won't be able to open it. Then maybe it won't matter that we don't have weapons."

"That's a good idea," Cole says, and Miranda feels a surge of pride.

She moves to the unit nearest the door. "Help me empty the shelves so it won't be as heavy." Amina and Cole move toward her, but Grace stays put. Miranda stands in front of her and holds out her hands. "Come on, Grace. Get up and help."

After a few seconds, Grace, still whimpering, grabs Miranda's hand and stands up.

"Maybe I can help too." Javier pushes himself up on his elbows.

"No, you can't, buddy," Cole says matter-of-factly. "Moving around is just going to make that wound bleed more."

Together Miranda, Grace, and Cole start dumping stacks of flannel shirts and boxes of chunky boots on the floor. Amina tries to neatly pile things. The shelves are made of lighter, flimsier metal than the framework of the shelving unit, so they leave them in place.

Miranda mouths the words "One, two, three," and then the four of them push at the same time. The shelving unit slides only a couple of inches. Without saying anything, they gradually figure out how to work together and the best places to push, skidding it a little farther with each shove. Once, it makes a loud metallic squeal and they all freeze. But when there's no answering noise from the far side of the door, they resume pushing.

And finally, they manage to slide it across the door.

"Good job!" Javier whispers. Amina mimes clapping. Grace tries on a trembling smile. Miranda can't help grinning.

Then Cole whispers a curse.

"What's the matter?" Miranda looks more closely at the door. No hinges, which means they must be on the other side. And that means . . . She swears too.

Amina's eyes fill with tears. Grace still looks confused until Miranda explains, "The door. It opens out."

NO MATTER
WHAT HAPPENS

4:17 P.M.

MIRANDA ROUNDS ON AMINA. "YOU work here," she says through gritted teeth. "You know which way the door closes! Why didn't you say something while we were busting our butts?"

Now all the killers need to do is yank open the door, poke one of their guns between the shelves, and spray the room.

Amina puts her hands on her hips. "Hey, it was your idea, not mine! I was pushing too. I just didn't think of it."

"Be quiet!" Cole puts his finger to his lips. "They'll hear you!"

Part of Miranda knows he's right, but another part welcomes the anger surging through her veins, burning off some of her terror. "Maybe she *wants* them to hear us. After all, she's the one in the hijab."

"What are you talking about?" Amina whispers.

Grace opens her eyes and looks back and forth between them.

"*Allahu akbar*, isn't that it?" Miranda says, "What Muslims say when they shoot people or blow up a bomb?"

Amina's eyes widen. "Did you hear someone saying that? It means God is great. Something no terrorists understand."

Rather than answer, Miranda looks away. That had been the terrifying thing. The shooters hadn't said anything. But why else would anyone do such a hateful thing?

"I'm as American as the rest of you. I'm sick of people calling me a terrorist just because I cover my hair. There's crazy people in every religion." Amina raises her chin. "And if I was part of it, why would *I* be trapped in here?"

"I didn't hear anyone saying anything about any kind of God." Cole closes his eyes and swallows. "But I'm sure those guys have some kind of agenda."

"Yeah," Javier says quietly. "They want to kill a lot of people. What difference does it make why they want to?"

"All right. I'm sorry," Miranda spits out. She moves back toward Javier. It's only a few steps, but by the time she reaches him her legs feel too weak to support her weight. She sinks down on the loose mat of sweaters. She was okay when she was helping him or trying to barricade the door. But her head replays a loop of horror. The blood blooming on Grace's mom's chest. The expression on the face of the lady with the red scarf when the bullet hit her. The curly-haired woman's legs churning against the blood-streaked floor until a shot stilled her forever.

How long will it be until everyone in this room is just as dead?

A touch on her hand makes her jerk, her heart hammering. But it's just Javier. He gives her hand a squeeze, then takes his away.

Miranda looks around the room. Cole is rubbing his face with his palms. Amina is biting her lip as she types on her phone. Tears roll down Grace's face as she mutters "Daddy" and "Mom," stabbing a button on her phone over and over.

Cole looks up. "What have you guys heard in the last few minutes?"

"You mean out there?" Miranda forces herself to think back. "Nothing. Not since that guy made those announcements."

"I think the killing has stopped. If people were still being shot, the cops would force their way in. But if they're not, the cops will try to negotiate."

How long could that take? The sweaters under Javier's leg are already splotched with red. He needs a better bandage than a couple of sweatshirts.

And Miranda knows just where she can find one.

She slips her hand under her loose sweater and inside the wide Ace bandage wrapped around her torso. No one's looking her way, so she pulls out the boxes of Clinique mascara and hides them under the pile of sweaters. When she straightens up, she sees that Javier is watching her, but his face doesn't hold any judgment.

Miranda does the math. If this hadn't happened, she would be on her way to Matthew now. If this hadn't happened, soon she would be handing over everything she stole in the past few days. Soon she would be feeling so much better. Or rather, she wouldn't be feeling anything at all. Instead, now she's in withdrawal. Shivering, she swipes at her nose with the back of her hand.

"Don't cry." Javier's the one with a bullet wound, but he's trying to console her.

"I'm not." Miranda's eyes are wet, but she's telling the truth. She tugs the Ace bandage free.

Suddenly, Grace raises her phone to her ear. Her face changes. "Daddy!"

Even as everyone signals her to keep her voice down, they all lean forward to listen.

Then the light in Grace's eyes dims and the joy leaves her voice. "Oh. Okay. Daddy, if you hear this message, first of all, I want you to know that I love you. Okay? I love you very much. I'm at Fairgate Mall in Portland. Oh, Daddy, there's men with guns and they're shooting people." Her voice cracks. "And . . . and . . . and Mom's dead. They killed her." She swallows. "And now I'm hiding with a bunch of people in a Culpeppers. In the storeroom." Her whisper is strangled. "And no matter what happens, just know that I love you and Emily so, so much." She hangs up, puts her hand over her eyes, and starts to cry again.

Cole moves closer and puts his arm around her shoulders. "I'm so sorry you're going through this."

"It's not your fault," she chokes out.

Grace's failure to connect is a fresh reminder of how alone they are. Miranda looks away from her naked pain. She feels so helpless, but maybe there's still something she can do. "Can one of you guys help me with Javier's leg? It's still bleeding."

Cole gives Grace's shoulder a squeeze before releasing her and coming over. He leans down. "How're you feeling, buddy?"

"Okay," Javier says. His hairline is beaded with sweat. After a pause, he adds, "I mean, it hurts."

"Try to stay calm." Cole's own voice is calm nearly to the point of disinterest. "The more stressed you get, the higher your blood pressure. Which makes you pump out more blood. If we had a field kit, I could dump some coagulants in the wound. But we've got nothing."

Cole sounds so knowledgeable. His hair seems too long, but . . . "Are you in the army or something?" Miranda asks.

"My brothers were." His voice falters, and he looks in the direction of the food court, his face contorting.

She doesn't ask any more. Doesn't want to know what that past tense means. Or how long it's been true.

On top of the desk is a sports water bottle. Cole undoes the cap and sniffs. "Water," he says, handing it to Javier. "Here. Take little sips every minute or two. Drinking is about the only way to replace the blood you've lost. But don't drink too much or too fast or you'll throw up."

Miranda holds up the Ace bandage. "Can you help me bandage his leg?"

Cole takes the length of tan elastic from her. "Why do you have this?"

"I hurt my ribs." Hopefully, Javier won't say anything about the mascara.

"I thought doctors didn't strap ribs anymore," Cole says. "It's bad for them to be immobile." When her only answer is a shrug, he turns to Javier. "Let's take a look at the wound first. Maybe we can pack it with something."

Cole takes the scissors from the desk and washes them in the bathroom. Returning, he pinches the cloth around the bullet hole on the front of Javier's thigh and then cuts out a circle. Javier holds himself still, his face shining with sweat.

Cole wipes the blood away with a sweater. The wound, which is toward the outside of his thigh, is not as scary as Miranda feared. About as wide as her pinky, it looks more like a puncture.

"That's got to be the entrance wound," Cole says. He spreads a clean sweater next to Javier's legs and then has him roll onto his belly. On the back, the wound is about the size of a nickel, with ragged edges. Even after Cole wipes it clean, blood wells up steadily. Both Amina and Grace look once, grimace, and then look away.

"You're super lucky it missed bone." Cole's words are cheerful, but his expression, which Javier can't see, is grim. "And that it went straight through." He looks at Amina. "Does the store sell anything clean and small I could pack the wound with to try to stop the bleeding?"

Amina scans the shelves. "Maybe we could cut up a scarf?"

Javier props himself on his elbows. "Do you have that thing for girls?"

Miranda and Amina exchange a puzzled glance.

"El tampón?" he ventures.

"He's right." Cole's low voice sparks with excitement.

64

"If we had one, we could use it to plug the bullet wound. It would probably stop the bleeding."

When neither of the other girls speaks, Miranda says, "Um, I've got one." She opens her purse and gets it out. Not meeting anyone's eyes, she starts to hand it to Cole.

He shakes his head. "We don't need another pair of hands touching it. Wash up first, and then, when you open it, only touch the applicator."

Oh no no no. "Can't *you* put it in?" Miranda says.

"We need to minimize the chance of contamination."

After a long pause, Miranda goes to wash her hands. For a few seconds, Javier's blood turns the water pink as it runs off her fingers. After it runs clear, she washes the ridiculous-looking makeup, now tear-streaked and smeared, from her face. She turns the water to cold and drinks it from her cupped hands.

In the mirror, her eyes look back at her from someone else's head. Who is this girl with dark circles under her eyes and blood smeared on her clothes?

Breaking her own gaze, Miranda turns the water to hot and scrubs her hands with soap. She waves her hand to get a paper towel, then carefully dries. Back out in the main part of the storeroom, she gets down on her knees and opens the wrapper.

"Just put it in slowly," Cole advises. To Javier he says, "Try to take deep breaths."

It's easier than she thought it would be to slide the plastic applicator into the exit hole. When it's about half-way in, Javier groans softly, and Miranda freezes. But Cole nods at her to keep going. Swallowing back nausea, she does, until only the string is showing, then pulls back the applicator.

Using the scissors, Cole cuts a flannel shirt into squares. Miranda and Amina help hold them in place while he binds them with Miranda's Ace bandage, which has a built-in Velcro edge. Grace does nothing more than watch, but at least she's no longer keening and muttering.

Javier rolls onto his back. "Thank you," he says softly. "Thank you, Cole and Miranda, Amina and Grace." He nods at each of them in turn.

Miranda has to look away. Will the things they did really matter? Or will Javier and everyone else end up just as dead as if they hadn't done anything?

THE ONE WHO DECIDES

PARKER TAKES ONE MORE STEP BACK INTO the Shoe Mill and out of sight of the killers. He lets his body make the decision. It's what makes him a good wrestler. If you wait until you've analyzed everything, you'll just end up getting pinned.

Besides, it's better to stay in his body, not his head. If he considered this logically, Parker would start screaming. He's just watched people die.

But he won't think about that. Instead, he focuses on finding Moxie. Finding his sister and saving her. He hasn't quite worked out the how. Maybe they can find someplace to hide, or maybe he'll discover an exit that the killers have overlooked. Or maybe he'll get really lucky and it will turn out that Moxie isn't locked in here at all but has somehow made it outside.

The killers might not be able to see him anymore, but some of the other hostages can. The people who aren't lined up against the doors sag along walls, or sit on benches or the floor. They've left a wide space around the dead man. People have begun to whisper to each other, and when that isn't met with shouts or gunfire, the talking becomes a low murmur. The college girls stand weeping with their arms around one another. Next to them, the mother of the little boy who was crying earlier is rocking him, her bound hands looped over his narrow back. Thankfully, he now looks half-asleep.

Parker's all the way inside the store now. The meaty scent of leather fills his nostrils. Still no sign of Moxie. But in the back, there's a curtain made of hanging vertical three-inch-wide gray rubber strips, the kind that separate when you walk through them. If Moxie's here, he thinks that's where he'll find her.

How long will it be until Lips ends up close enough to see inside the store? Parker's afraid to turn away from the entrance, so instead he shuffles backward. His heart stutters when one of those little benches the salespeople sit on catches him in the calves. He stumbles, but manages to keep his balance.

Finally, the rubber strips that dangle all the way to the floor brush his shoulder blades. He takes one more step back, the strips parting. Then he's on the other side.

Something cold presses against his temple. His blood turns to ice.

"Don't make a sound," a man whispers in his ear, his breath sour. Parker moves only his eyes. Standing between the shelves of shoe boxes is the guy with the shaved head, the one he first saw behind the pillar.

Parker raises his zip-tied hands and then risks a

whisper. "I just want to find my sister. She's seven and wearing a red coat."

The other man shrugs one shoulder. His expressionless face gleams with sweat. "Haven't seen her." He gestures with his chin. "What's going on out there?"

"We're all trapped between the doors and that security gate they pulled across. One of them is inside the gate, and two are outside. All of them have automatic rifles. They made some people press up against the doors, facing out. It's supposed to make the police think twice about coming in." Parker looks at the guy's shaved head and the jacket straining against his biceps. "Are you a cop?"

"No." He doesn't offer any other explanation.

"What're you going to do? You have to stop them before they kill anyone else."

The other man answers through gritted teeth. "Be realistic. If I go out there, I'll just get mowed down. I might get one—or maybe, if I'm really lucky, two—but there's at least three of them." He shakes his head. "I'm going to stay put. This way, I control the space, not them. And if anyone comes in, I'll be the one who decides who lives or dies." He nudges the back of Parker's head with the side of the gun. "So go on, get out of here. And good luck finding your sister. If I were you, once you do, I would try and find your own space to hide. Out there, you're just one of the herd. And they're looking for animals to cull."

4:24 p.m.

SKINNER: Oh Jesus God, he's making all the male hostages lie down on the floor on their bellies in a line.

DISPATCH: How many hostages?

SKINNER: About a dozen. I think he's going to kill them. Like an execution!

DISPATCH: 68, RP says one gunman is making male hostages lie down. He thinks they're planning to execute them.

UNIT 68: We need the Crisis Negotiation Team stat.

DISPATCH: Copy.

WHAT YOU NEED TO DO

4:24 P.M.

WHEN MIRANDA'S PHONE BUZZES, SHE jerks. It's her dad. In her chest, a bubble of hope expands. If anyone can fix this mess, it's him. He travels all over the world. He buys failing businesses and turns them around. He's even had dinner alone with the president. Twice.

She forgets to whisper. "Daddy?"

"Shh!" Amina puts her finger against her lips. Javier holds up a cautioning hand. Cole frowns. Only Grace seems unconcerned.

"Honey! Where are you? Are you all right? Did you get out?"

She has been holding it together until now. But at the sound of his voice, her head fills with water. Her heart feels squeezed by a fist.

For a moment, she can't speak at all. Finally, she manages a strangled whisper. "No. I'm still in Culpeppers. I mean, we are. There's five of us, including me."

"Let me talk for a second to whoever's in charge."

Her dad still doesn't get it. No one's in charge, there're no adults, and you have to figure out how to survive using just what you have.

"Everyone here is about my age," Miranda says as she looks around the room. Javier's biting his lip. Grace is trembling. Amina's fingering the edge of her scarf, her mouth turned down at the corners. Cole's face looks like it's chiseled out of stone. "We tried to leave through the service corridor, but there was shooting back there, too. We pulled down the metal shutter at the front of the store, but I guess that won't really stop bullets, so we're hiding in the storeroom."

"That's a good idea," he says. "A very good idea." For a second, the compliment makes Miranda forget where she is. Between his business trips and the new baby twins, it's been at least a month since she's talked to him. "You need to keep as much space as you can between you and the bad guys." His voice is muffled as he speaks to someone else, but then he comes back to her. "Culpeppers. What stores is that next to? They're still working on getting blueprints."

She tries to remember. "I think we're between LA Nails and a Gymboree. On the other side of the food court from Nordstrom."

"Do you know how many shooters there are? The guy I've been talking with is trying to verify that information."

"They were firing down into the food court." She has to swallow before she can keep talking. "Maybe four or five?"

"Okay. I'll pass that along. They're holding at least

two dozen hostages. They've locked the exits, and they've got hostages lined up against the glass doors."

Is that where Parker is? "When I saw the bike locks on the doors, I got out of there right away."

"That's my girl. You thought on your feet. In your text, you said someone was bleeding?"

"Yeah. One guy here was shot in the leg." She exchanges a look with Javier. "But I think we got it stopped."

"Okay." His voice thickens. "Miranda, I am so proud of you. Keep doing what you need to do to survive, okay?" His voice fades to a whisper. "And put yourself first. You take care of Miranda, and let the others watch after themselves."

Glad she hadn't risked putting him on speakerphone, Miranda says only, "Okay."

"There's something you need to know. I'm hearing they're going to send in a SWAT team soon to take out the shooters. Do you know what a flash bang is?"

"Some kind of grenade?"

"Yeah, but it doesn't actually blow anything up. It just makes a loud noise and a bright light. It stuns people. So if you hear an explosion, don't worry. It will be giving the SWAT team the cover they need to end this."

"Okay."

"I'll make sure they know exactly where you are, but you have to stay put until they have taken care of these animals. Wait until you hear the police saying it's safe to come out. You don't want to get caught in any cross fire."

She takes a shuddery breath, then repeats, "Okay."

"And I'm going to get there. I'll be waiting outside for you."

It kills Miranda to think her dad is so near. She wants nothing more than to be wrapped in his arms, to cry on his chest, to feel like a little kid again.

"I love you so much, Daddy." She doesn't want to say good-bye. It's too final. Instead she chokes out, "See you soon."

As soon as she disconnects, the tears come flooding out. Everyone is looking at her contorted face, listening to her weird, strangled noises. Miranda tries to wipe her nose on her sleeve, but it's no use. She's an ugly mess.

A slender arm encircles her shoulder. It's Grace, her face as sad as Miranda feels. And then Amina is on the other side, offering one of the store's scarves. Even Javier is patting her foot.

"What did he say?" Cole asks.

"A SWAT team's going to set off some flash bangs to surprise the killers, and then they're going to take them out. We need to stay put so we don't get caught in the cross fire."

"Why is SWAT going to do that? In the middle of nego-tiating?" Cole looks angry.

"They're gonna kill them." Javier snorts. "And they deserve it."

Cole swipes his hand over his face. "And when is this supposed to happen?"

"Soon," Miranda says.

Amina's full lips stretch into something like a smile.

Grace raises a clenched fist. "They deserve to die for what they did to my mom." A reddish-purple bruise circles her wrist like a bracelet.

Wincing, Javier points. "Ouch—did I do that?"

Miranda remembers yanking at Grace's wrist to keep her from leaving. The bruise is probably her fault.

Grace covers her wrist with her other hand and pulls it to her chest. "I bruise easy." Her blouse hangs so loose, it's like it's on a hanger instead of a body. She can't weigh much more than a hundred pounds. A lot of girls at Miranda's school say you can never be too skinny or too rich. Grace, in her five-hundred-dollar size-zero jeans, looks like she's taken it too far. She probably lives on baby carrots and iceberg lettuce.

Amina must be thinking about food too, because her stomach lets out a loud gurgle. The unexpected sound breaks the tension. Miranda starts to giggle. Javier joins in, and then Grace, although her laugh has an edge of hysteria. The more they try to keep quiet, the harder it is not to make noise. Even Cole wears a half smile.

Amina looks mortified. She whispers, "I was about to have my lunch. Then everything happened."

"That sounds nice," Grace says wistfully. "Something normal."

"It's still here." Amina gets to her feet. "Do you guys want to split it? It's stew and bread."

With no Oxy left in her system, Miranda feels more like throwing up than eating, but everyone else either shrugs or nods.

Amina comes back from her locker with a wide-mouthed thermos and a small brown paper bag. After opening the bag, she tears off pieces of flatbread pocked with black scorch marks and passes them around.

Years ago, back when Miranda's family was still a family, they used to go to church. The first Sunday of the month, they took communion: a tiny glass of grape juice and a pale papery wafer plucked from a passed plate. Like then, this bread seems as if it could be magical. Like a sign they will make it. Despite her queasiness, Miranda takes a half-dollar-size piece and lets it rest on her tongue. It tastes of flour and corn meal and char. Miraculously, her stomach doesn't rebel. Eventually she chews and swallows.

Meanwhile, Amina hands the thermos to Cole. He peers down, looking dubious. "I thought you said it was stew."

"It is. It's a Somali stew." Amina raises her chin. "*Sahan ful*. Fava beans with tomato sauce."

He lifts the white plastic spoon to his lips, but at the first taste his expression smooths out. "This is really good."

After two bites, he hands the thermos to Miranda. The smell of ginger, cloves, and chiles overwhelms her temporary truce with her stomach. After hastily handing the thermos to Grace, she leans closer to Amina and whispers, "I'm sorry, my stomach's just upset." She swallows and adds, "And I'm sorry I suggested it was Muslims who are doing this."

"It's not the first time someone's implied I'm a terrorist just because I wear a hijab." Amina raises her dark eyes to Miranda's. "I was born here. I'm just as much an American as you are."

Before Miranda can come up with an answer, Grace

says, "Excuse me, but do you know if these beans are organically grown?"

Amina and Miranda share an amused/annoyed glance, and the tension between them breaks. "I have no idea," Amina says with a shrug.

Grace hesitates, then digs in the spoon. Her eyebrows go up. "Yum. That's spicy, but in a good way."

Javier offers Grace his water and she takes a couple of sips. As she hands it back, he says, "You guys, when this is over and the police come, I might try to take off."

"Why?" Grace asks.

"I don't need to be answering too many questions."

Miranda still doesn't understand. Then Cole says, "He means he's in this country illegally. Am I right, buddy?" There's a new edge to his voice.

Javier doesn't flinch. "I've been here since I was a baby, but you're right, I'm not legal."

"I thought," Amina says hesitantly, "you could stay if you were under sixteen when your parents brought you."

"That's only true if you've stayed in the States for the whole time." Javier sighs. "But last year I lived for nine months with my *abuela* in Mexico. My grandmother. She was dying, and I took care of her. But that means I don't qualify. If Immigration finds out, I'll get deported."

Cole's lips twist. "Maybe that's for the best. People like you are taking Americans' jobs."

Javier's face hardens. "People like me are taking jobs no Americans want. All day, I clean up people's garbage. Sometimes dirty diapers and vomit. If Americans want my job so much, how come no one's applying for the openings we have?"

Cole just grunts and looks away. The good mood begun by Miranda's dad's phone call and Amina's food evaporates. No one is looking at each other.

All that's left is to wait for the cops to save them. To wait for it to be over.

ONE LAST TIME

A T THE ENTRANCE TO THE SHOE MILL, Parker peeps out. Lips is talking through the gate to Mole and Wolf. Seeing them, he rages silently against the guy with the gun. How hard would it be to kill them all right now? He could probably take them out before they could react.

When the killers are all looking the other way, Parker slips out of the store.

He's about ready to check out the AT&T store when he looks across the hall. How could he have been so stupid? If Moxie is trapped in here, he knows exactly where she is.

Keeping clumps of people between him and the killers, he slowly moves toward the Van Duyn candy store. He ducks inside. A section of the white counter has been flipped up. He checks behind the cash registers. No Moxie. With his bound hands, he eases open the door at the back of the shop. Once he's inside what turns out to be a small workroom, he uses his foot to gently close the door behind him.

At first, the room appears to be empty. His heart sinks. Then he takes another step and catches a glimpse of red. Moxie is tucked on the far side of the marble worktable that sits in the center of the room. Judging by the empty brown paper candy cups strewn around her, she has polished off at least a dozen candies.

From behind the finger he holds to his lips, Parker whispers, "Moxie!"

"Parker!" Her eyes go wide. She jumps to her feet and hugs him. With his hands bound, he can't return the hug. When her slender arms go around his waist, his eyes get wet. He angrily blinks away the tears. Why couldn't his little sister be outside and safe? Instead she is only a few yards away from a dead man and killers with guns.

When she steps back, she tilts her head. "What's happening, Parker? Why are you tied up?"

He taps his finger against his lips again. "We need to be really quiet, Moxie. There are bad men outside. Did you see them?"

"I wanted a free candy sample, and then there was all these loud noises!" She holds her hands over her ears to demonstrate. "Everybody started running. The candy lady pushed me in here and said I had to be quiet and hide. And she said I could have all the candy I wanted."

Moxie's only experience with death has been a robin that bounced off their living room's floor-to-ceiling windows that look out over Lake Oswego. That day, she begged Parker to make the suddenly boneless bird fly again. How will she react when she sees what's outside this room?

He can't let that happen.

His eyes go to the marble-topped worktable. It holds empty gold cardboard boxes of various sizes, white wrapping paper, and stacks of ruffled brown paper cups. And a large knife, presumably for cutting up samples.

If he cuts his zip ties and the killers find out, they'll kill him. Screw it. He grabs the knife and manages to slide the blade, pointing toward him, between his wrists. With a few contortions, he saws through one of the loops. A few seconds later, he's free.

Now that he's found Moxie, what should he do? Going back into the hall is clearly not a good option. He has to keep her as far away as possible from the men with guns.

He turns in a circle. The ceiling is made of white acoustical tiles held on metal rails. Even if he could get her up there, the tiles don't look strong enough to hold Moxie's fifty pounds.

What about the cabinets under the counter? He opens a door, revealing boxes of candy. The shelves are about eighteen inches apart, a couple of feet deep, and maybe about four feet wide. Even if he wanted to hide there, there's no way he'd fit. But Moxie's built like a sprite.

"Okay, Moxie, right now we're going to play a game. We need to hide even better from the bad guys. And if we are really, really quiet, they won't catch us."

"I'm good at hiding," Moxie offers.

"That's why you get to hide first," Parker says. "But you can't come out unless you hear me tell you to." He imagines a future where he's dead. "Or the police. But no one else."

He can see Moxie thinking about this, her head tilted to one side. What are the chances that she will actually stay hidden, that she won't get bored and come out, even if he leaves her with a stash of candy?

And then Parker thinks of a solution, because it's the same trick that always works on him. "Forget it," he says, turning away. "I don't think you can do it. The minute you get in the cupboard, you're going to want to get out again. Or you'll make a noise. You're not old enough. You're not patient enough."

She tugs at his hand. "I *can* do it. I'll be really, really quiet. I'll be like a teensy little mouse." She pinches her lips closed.

He eyes her, his expression fake-dubious, which echoes his real internal doubts. His mom always talks about sugar highs. How long until Moxie is literally bouncing off the walls?

Still, he opens the cupboards, and pushes boxes out of the way, and has her slither back on her belly.

"Okay. Now it's time to make it so that no one can see you." He begins stacking boxes in front of her, starting at her feet. If it were him, he'd feel claustrophobic, but she doesn't make a sound, just watches him with her bright blue eyes.

"But where are you going to hide, Parker?"

"Oh, don't worry. I've got a really good place picked out."

Her brows draw together. "But where?"

"It's a secret," he says, putting a last stack of walnut fudge in front of her face. As soon as he does, he's sorry that he hasn't kissed her or touched her one last time. "Are you good in there?" He tries to keep his voice from sounding strangled.

"Yeah," she whispers.

"And remember, don't come out until you hear me or the cops, okay?"

"Okay."

He thinks of another tactic to keep her hidden. "I'll bet you that I am the better hider. I'll bet you five dollars."

"I'm going to win!" Her voice is muffled by the boxes.

"We'll see about that."

He starts to close the cupboard door, then worries that won't leave enough fresh air. He leaves it ajar a careful half inch, then picks up all the wrappers and puts them in the trash. He doesn't want any of the killers coming in and wondering where the person who ate them went. The papers are so light, as flimsy as his and Moxie's chances of surviving this.

The door to the workroom doesn't have a lock. But he won't go back outside. Instead, he turns off the light and settles himself in the corner behind the door. In his hand, he clutches the knife.

THE BIGGEST SECRET EVER

IN CULPEPPERS'S STOREROOM, NO ONE IS talking. Grace is back to whimpering and rocking. Amina is checking her phone. Javier and Cole both have their eyes closed. Javier's face is twisted with pain, while Cole looks exhausted, his head tipped back against the wall.

Miranda's eyes are drawn to her photo thumbtacked to the bulletin board above Cole's head. She's one of a couple of dozen sullen faces. After Amina caught Miranda, she grabbed her wrist when she tried to run. Amina isn't that big, but her grip was like a ring of iron.

And this was where Amina took her. This very same room. When she was here a month ago, Miranda thought it was all going to end. Finally. She would be arrested and her parents would find out about everything. The lying. The stealing. And the rest. She was filled with shame, but also relief. Instead of calling the police, though, Amina snapped Miranda's photo and then banned her from the store. Back then, Miranda told herself that she was lucky.

And she hasn't gone near Culpeppers since, at least not until today.

Now her head hurts worse than it had when she was trying to get coffee, which was when? She checks her phone: not even an hour ago. Earlier she was freezing, and now sweat is pouring off her. Yesterday, Matthew called off their meeting without explanation. If this whole nightmare hadn't happened, she would have met him by now. He would have traded her some Oxy for the items she stole, and right about now she would be starting to feel good again.

Last summer, OxyContin started showing up at parties. It was a prescription drug, made in a factory someplace. That meant it was safe.

And the first time Miranda took it? It had been like falling in love. Like figuring out the biggest secret ever. She still remembers sitting in the backyard of some guy she went to school with, his parents gone and a party all around her, a party where normally she would have felt anxious the whole time. It was Matthew—Matthew Scout, although she didn't know his full name then—who had given her that first pill. It wasn't long before euphoria filled her. Miranda felt energized and mellow at the same time. It wasn't like pot, which made her paranoid. Or alcohol, which made her talk too much and then made her cry. Oxy just made her feel good. A half hour after swallowing that first pill, she had been relaxing against Matthew's shoulder.

It turned out that lots of people in her high school play around with Oxy. People from every sort of group—the burnouts, the geniuses, and even the girls who were wicked-good softball players who were going to get college scholarships—they've all tried it. But only the rich kids have the money to keep doing it, which makes it more cool. Because it's so expensive, this big rich drug.

The one problem is that even though Miranda lives in tony Lake Oswego, she isn't all that rich. Hasn't been since her dad left her mom. Her dad still buys her things, but he doesn't give her that much cash. And Matthew might have handed her that first pill free, as a favor, but he couldn't afford to keep doing that.

And that was before he showed her that if you crushed up the pills and snorted them, you felt even better. And the next thing Miranda knew, if she didn't have any in her system, she felt terrible. She cashed seven thousand dollars in savings bonds her aunts had given her for birthdays, money meant for college. She sold her phone and told her dad she lost it. She sold her leather jacket. She sold her mom's camera, which hadn't been used since the divorce. Matthew knows someone who has an eBay store, so Miranda has started shoplifting the things he says sell well. Anything just to stay in that happy place. Plus, it turns out that if you stop using, you feel worse than you ever have in your life. Like you have a fever. Like you're going to start vomiting and never stop. Like your bones are being broken. Like she feels now.

"There's a fix for that," Matthew has told her. "You could just start using heroin. It's way cheaper." He does it himself and says it's no big deal.

But so far Miranda has been saying no. If you use needle drugs, then you really *are* an addict.

"Look at this," Amina whispers, and shows Grace something on her phone. At least it stops Grace from not-quite-silently crying.

Miranda pulls out her own phone. She texts Parker.

R U out? Hiding w/ people at Culpeppers.

A few weeks ago, down in his basement, he had offered her a trade. Her time for his money. And she let him do whatever he wanted, knowing it would eventually make the pounding in her head go away.

Is Parker even alive to read her text? Probably not. When she shifts, she can smell herself, the acrid scent of fear. Miranda swallows hard against a roil of nausea.

Dear God, she prays, not even certain there is anyone to listen, *help me. Help us.*

WHAT THEY WANT ME TO BELIEVE

A WHISPER FROM AMINA BREAKS THE silence. "Shouldn't SWAT be here by now?"

Miranda, who has been texting back and forth with Parker, checks her phone. It's been nearly a half hour since she talked to her dad. "He didn't say exactly when."

"What if they don't come?" Amina asks. "What if they're never coming?"

Miranda feels just as itchy and anxious, and it's not only from the lack of Oxy. "Maybe we need to find another way out of here." She points up at a rectangular vent set just under the white acoustical tile ceiling. "What about that?"

Javier squints. "I don't think anyone could really fit in there."

Cole also looks dubious. "That's the kind of thing that only works in movies."

"It's still worth a try," Miranda insists, even though part of her thinks they're probably right. But they can't just sit here waiting forever.

"I'm going to trade you," she says to Javier, pulling out

the bottom desk drawer. "Put your feet on this and let me have the chair."

After raising the chair to its highest position, Miranda pushes the computer aside. With a grunt, she lifts the chair onto the desk.

"Can you hold it still for me?" she asks Cole.

After he grabs it, she clambers up on the desk, puts one knee on the seat, and then stands on the chair, touching the wall for balance. The bottom of the vent is now even with the top of her head. Tugging the grate free, she hands it down to Amina as she measures the space with her eyes. This close, it does look too small. Javier's probably right. But she doesn't want to give up.

Amina and Cole are on their feet, watching her. Javier's propped up on his elbows, doing the same. Grace sits with her eyes closed, lost in her own little world.

Amina's shorter and wider than Miranda. Even though Cole's lanky, his shoulders are broad. Javier's short and sturdy, and then there's his leg.

But Grace is as thin as a thread.

And even if only one of them can escape through the air ducts, isn't that better than none of them?

"Grace!" Miranda whispers, but the other girl doesn't even twitch. "Grace!"

Cole nudges Grace with his foot, and that gets through.

With dull eyes, she looks up at Miranda. "What?"

"I'm not tall enough to see inside the vent. Can you trade places with me and look?"

"I guess."

After Miranda gets down, she helps Grace take her

place. Under her hands, Grace's body feels stringy, just skin and bones and tendons.

Grace braces her hands flat inside the vent and then hops. She shakes her head. "It's too dark in there. I can't see."

There're flashlights on phones, but Grace is going to need to brace both hands to jump. Even if she sets the phone down inside, it probably won't light all the way to the end of the duct.

Miranda gets an idea. "Put your phone in flashlight mode and then try using your headband to hold it on your forehead. You know, like a miner's lamp."

"Okay." Grace digs in her jeans pocket for her phone. Is there the tiniest spark of life in her eyes?

Grace presses the phone against her forehead with one hand and, with the other, pulls the headband over it. It works. For the first time, she smiles. Then she braces her hands flat inside the duct and jumps. But when she tries to pull herself up and in, there's a metallic bang.

Worse than that, the space is clearly too small. Grace's head and one shoulder fit inside the vent, but the other shoulder gets stuck outside, leaving her at a slant. Her feet kick in midair. Miranda grabs one ankle and guides her foot back onto the chair.

"Even if you could fit in there, they would definitely hear you moving around," Amina says. "Then they would just shoot the ceiling."

The light has left Grace's eyes. "It doesn't matter. At the end, there's just a big fan." She climbs down off the desk.

"Hey, what's *that*?" Javier touches his own shoulder while looking at Grace's.

They all follow his gaze. Getting stuck in the vent pushed Grace's blouse down over her right shoulder. A Band-Aid half dangles from her skin, exposing a round, flat reddish lump just under her collarbone. The lump is topped with a half-healed incision. It looks like someone has inserted something the size of a large button just under her pale skin. Miranda's already touchy stomach does another flip. It doesn't just *look* like that. It *is* that.

Flushing, Grace pulls her blouse back up. "Nothing."

"It doesn't look like nothing." Javier raises one eyebrow.

"It's a chemo port," Cole says with authority.

"Oh my God," Miranda whispers, "Grace, do you have cancer?"

"I don't." Grace's lips twist. "That's just what they want me to believe. But I don't even feel sick." Her fingers rise to the side of her neck. "I just had this stupid lump on my neck—you know, just a random swollen lymph node. Like from mono or the flu. But they said it's Hodgkin's lymphoma. And they *made* me get this"—she touches the spot through her blouse—"so they can pump chemicals straight into my veins."

"My mom had one of those," Cole says. "She got lung cancer even though she never smoked."

"Then you know how they treat cancer." Grace fixes her gaze on him. "Poisoning. Burning. Cutting. They basically try to kill you and hope that the cancer dies first."

"When my mom got sick," Cole says, "we did every-thing the doctors said to. Chemo, surgery, radiation. It all just made her worse. By the time she died, she weighed seventy-nine pounds. She didn't even look like a person. She looked like a baby bird with a broken neck." He closes his eyes.

Amina winces. "But a lot of people recover from cancer. And if the treatment lets you live . . ."

"But it's not even a matter of dying. I'm not going to *die*." Grace shakes her head in disbelief. "My m"—she makes herself say the word—"mom found this place in Mexico that treats you with plants. We were on our way there. It's like ancient wisdom that works with your body, not against it. Chemo really messes you up inside. First of all, you lose your hair."

"But hair grows back," Amina points out.

"That's easy for you to say." Grace runs her fingers through her glossy brown hair, looking at Amina's headscarf. "But that's not even the important thing. If I did it, I probably could never have a baby. I'm only six-teen. I have a little sister. I love kids. Someday I want to be a mom."

If you're dead, you definitely can't be a mom, Miranda thinks. Still, it *is* Grace's life. "It's your body," she says. "You should be able to make choices about it."

"Exactly! But when I said I didn't want all those chemi-cals, the doctors kept insisting I'd probably be dead within two years. And that I would have a ninety-five percent chance of surviving if I did chemo." She makes a face. "But of course they don't make any money if you go to Mexico. My mom has been doing a lot of reading. Companies can't patent natural cures. Which means they can't make any money off them. Doctors won't get rich telling patients to drink milk thistle tea."

Miranda says slowly, "So you think that all the doctors and hospitals and drug companies know there's a better way to treat cancer but they're not telling anyone because they want to make money?" Some, maybe, but all of them? She doesn't believe that.

Grace shrugs. "Most of them probably just believe whatever they're told, the same as the rest of us."

Cole has been nodding. "All those companies that make drugs and chemicals—they want to keep us in the dark. Fighter jets are dumping chemtrails into the atmosphere. The Zika virus came from a government lab. Chicken is full of hormones. And the government covers it all up. My brothers were in the army. What you read in the papers or see on the news—half of it's wrong or flat made up."

"Exactly!" Grace bobs her head.

Are Grace and Cole right? Miranda doesn't want to believe it, but what about drugs like Oxy? The companies that make it must know how many people are using it the way she is, which isn't exactly for physical pain. Except now that it's completely out of her system, she really *is* in pain. Her joints ache fiercely, like someone is holding the ends of her bones and twisting them.

"That's why I want to try something natural," Grace says. "But the judge said I wasn't mature enough to make that decision. Even though my parents researched it."

"Wait a second." Javier looks at her. "Is this what you want or what your parents want?"

"It's what I want, of course," Grace says. "Do you think I want to lose my hair? Or not to be able to have kids?"

"That would still be better than dying," Amina says stubbornly.

"That's not the choice. Don't you see that? They tried to make it out that I didn't understand, but they're the ones who don't. The hospital went to a judge. And he ordered me to have surgery to put in this port, and then this week they were going to force me to do chemo. So my mom and me, we left Seattle. Dyed our hair, gave ourselves different names, withdrew a bunch of cash, and started driving. And now she's dead." Grace takes a deep, shuddering breath. "And I don't know what to do." She puts her hands over her face and starts to sob. "I just don't know what to do."

4:48 p.m.

SKINNER: Oh my God!

DISPATCH: Ron? What's happening?

SKINNER: No, no, no!

DISPATCH: Ron, take a deep breath and tell me what's going on.

SKINNER: Those male hostages they've got all lined up—they just shot one in the back of the head!

DISPATCH: Security guard reports at least one of the hostages has been shot.

UNIT 68: What's the ETA on SWAT? Or the Crisis Negotiation Team?

DISPATCH: Due to traffic, ETA ten for mobile command center. Longer for Crisis Negotiation.

UNIT 68: Copy. We can't wait. I've got a shield, a Halligan tool, and some flash bangs in my car. Give me three units for an active shooter. We have to go in.

DISPATCH: Copy. 43, 41, and 19. Respond to south parking lot of Fairgate Mall for active shooter.

UNIT 68: Get the RP to tell us the best way in.

DISPATCH: Ron, check your cams. What's the best entrance for our team to take?

SKINNER: I can't believe this. Everyone's dying!

DISPATCH: Ron, listen to me. We need to know where the officers can enter to help those people. Look at your cams.

SKINNER: I think they can come through Nordstrom. It looks empty.

WHO HE REALLY IS

PARKER'S NOT SURE HOW LONG HE'S BEEN waiting inside the Van Duyn workroom. His shoulders ache from pressing against the wall on one side and the door on the other. Moxie is, he thinks, asleep. There hasn't been even a rustle from the cupboard. And no sounds outside this room either, no matter how he strains to hear. No shouts. No gunshots. Even the sirens that were faintly wailing when the siege first started seem to have ceased.

While he waited for the killers to come through the door, and hoped that they never did, Parker set down the knife and pulled his phone from his back pocket. He'd missed a couple of dozen texts. From his mom, his dad, his friends. It looked like everyone else who was at his table managed to get out.

But the text that first caught his eye was Miranda's. **R U out? Hiding w/ people at Culpeppers.**

He texted her back. **Hiding Van Duyn storeroom w/ sister.**

30+ ppl trapped in hall. Killers pulled metal gate across. Already shot 1.

Thinking of Miranda fills him with deep shame. In fact, as he sits on this white tile floor and waits to see if he's going to die, Parker is ashamed by pretty much everything he's done recently. If he's honest with himself, he's turned into kind of a jerk, especially since the wrestling team took state. Today especially. Ignoring Moxie. Leaving a mess. Taunting that busboy. If there's a heaven, he's pretty sure that's not where he's going to end up.

But it's been going on for longer than just today. Like that one afternoon a few weeks ago that he spent with Miranda. He's surprised she cared enough to text, let alone to try to drag him to safety. He pictures her cowering behind Culpeppers's metal roll-down shutter, reviewing her life the way he's reviewing his.

A few weeks ago, Miranda had seemed to be the solution to a problem. Everyone always thought Parker was such a player. That he was getting some left, right, and center. The truth was that he had never done any of the things they thought. Nothing more than a few drunken kisses. And when he looked around school, it seemed like even the loneliest, ugliest losers were still managing to hook up.

If the talk turned to sex, Parker said as little as possible, trying to let a smirk and a shrug hint at his imaginary expertise. And because Parker was a golden boy, people believed it. A few girls even let people think that something had gone on between them. But the more his reputation grew, the more his confidence shrank. What if some girl expected something from him that he didn't even know how to do?

He and Miranda grew up only two blocks apart. The school boundary, however, falls between their houses. During summers when they were little, they played at the same park while their moms sat on a bench and gossiped. But as they got older, they saw each other less and less.

Then Parker had run into Miranda at a party, begging people for Oxy or, failing that, money for Oxy. Hinting that she would do anything for more of those round yellow pills.

Parker saw an opening. They could help each other out. And keep their mouths shut afterward.

He arranged for her to come over the next day after school, when his parents were at work and Moxie was on a playdate. Even though they were alone, he still started at every noise. Everything was both fake and too real.

Now, as he cradles his phone, the only light in the dark storeroom, Parker asks himself what he expected to feel after. Taller? Überconfident? Able to get with any girl he wanted?

But really he just wishes it had never happened. He gave her an extra hundred to make sure she kept it a secret. Still, he was worried. What if she laughed about him with those druggie friends of hers? What if she told people the truth?

Because the truth is that he doesn't know any more

than he did before that afternoon. He doesn't know what would make Miranda smile, let alone gasp.

It wasn't like he did anything bad to her. That's what Parker has told himself until today. She just lay there, but she didn't say no. She didn't say anything at all. Just closed her eyes and let him do whatever he wanted. Maybe it would have been better if he'd been drunk. Or she had one of those Oxys floating through her system, making her mellow and loose.

Now he sees himself for who he really is. There's not much he can do to fix things, but . . .

He sends another text to Miranda. **I'm really sorry for what happened. Sorry for everything.**

People aren't going to come to his funeral and say Parker was such a stud. If he's lucky, they might say he died trying to save his sister. If he's not lucky, they'll talk about all the times he's been a jerk.

Because he's been a bad guy way more times than he's been a good one.

It's okay, Miranda texts back. **Neither one of us was our best self that day.**

"Best self." He likes that thought. Like being better is still possible.

A sudden metallic bang, like someone just hammered on a piece of sheet metal, makes him jump. And it didn't come from out in the corridor, but instead from high on the other side of one of the workroom walls. He holds perfectly still, but all he hears is some faint scrabbling.

He unfreezes long enough to text Miranda. **Did u hear that bang?**

Someone here tried to get out thru vent. Too small.

Even though it's not even an avenue of escape that he thought of, the news makes Parker feel like another weight has been placed on his heart. They're never going to get out of here.

He tries to envision the mall's layout, to picture where Culpeppers and Van Duyn are and where their storerooms might lie in relation to each other.

I think ur on other side of my wall, he texts Miranda.

So near yet so far, she texts back, with some ridiculous smiley face sporting a hat and a beard. He's not even sure what it's supposed to mean, but it still makes his lips twitch, before he remembers how alone he is.

Parker is sitting on his heels, trying to write a text to his parents, backspacing and deleting and searching for the right words while snuffling back tears, when another text from Miranda pops up.

Hang tight. My dad said SWAT team coming.

When? he texts back. Is it really possible they might survive this?

Soon. He said stay hidden so we don't get shot by accident.

OK. Thx, Parker replies, then goes back to trying to find the right words to text his parents. But maybe he doesn't need to make them perfect. Maybe he'll be able to talk to them instead. Maybe he'll . . .

101

Suddenly a loud noise fills the air as something shoves him from behind. Parker is thrown onto his hands and knees.

And the knife is behind him, out of reach.

PEOPLE LIKE YOU

MIRANDA'S HEADACHE HAS GOTTEN worse as her body falls deeper into withdrawal. It's like she's in a cartoon, like her skull's pulsing with every beat of her heart. Javier is lying with his arm over his eyes. In the corner, Cole and Grace are talking quietly. Even if they are trading their favorite conspiracy theories, Miranda's just glad Grace has stopped crying. Amina is hunched over her phone, her thumbs flickering.

So is Miranda. She's answered messages from her friends. And from her mom, who's freaking out. Miranda's been angry at her for so long, but now that's melted away. For the last half hour, they've been texting variations of "I love you" back and forth. Miranda figures if those end up being her last words, they're pretty good ones.

She's also been messaging with Parker. What happened a few weeks ago was both their fault. Each of them thinking they were using the other to get what they wanted. Leaving both of them with less than when they started. Afterward, Miranda tried to tell herself it had been worth it. And when she swallowed that next yellow pill, it even felt kind of true. Still, until today she has hated both herself and Parker for what happened.

Coming so close to death has helped her to let go. To forgive. To be thankful that, at least as of right now, she and the others hiding are all still alive.

And SWAT will come soon. She holds tight to the thought.

Can't wait to get out of here, she texts Parker.

His reply comes a second later. **So you can forget?**

No. So I can remember.

"Who are you texting?" Javier asks. He's taken off his apron and rolled it up and is now using it as a pillow.

"My friend Parker." She points in the direction she thinks he is. "He's in the Van Duyn workroom with his sister. The killers bike-locked the doors shut. He says they pulled some kind of metal gate across the open end of the hall and trapped everyone."

Amina blows air through pursed lips. "I saw some guy in a hard hat installing that folding gate last week. I didn't even wonder why."

"You can do pretty much anything if you look official," Cole says. "If you wear a lanyard and carry a clipboard, no one asks too many questions."

A text from Matthew pops up. In her mind's eye, Miranda sees him: sleepy blue eyes, long dark hair caught up in a man bun, a trace of stubble on his jaw. When he holds her in his muscled arms, he's tall enough that she can tuck her head under his chin. She loves that feeling.

Where r u babe?

She was supposed to be at his apartment about a half hour ago.

Hiding in Fairgate. OK so far.

???

Haven't you heard the news? But Matthew's not exactly a news kind of guy. The only current events he keeps up on are the street prices for various drugs.

No.

Bunch of people shot at mall. I'm OK. 5 of us hiding in Culpeppers. SWAT coming.

r u joking?

Sadly, no.

His next text is a four-letter word, and then nothing more. Miranda waits for a declaration of love, or at least an expression of anxiety, but there is none. Maybe Matthew just can't get in touch with his feelings.

Or maybe they don't go much past vague annoyance at this disruption to his routine.

Despite how much her head hurts, Miranda realizes she's seeing things more clearly than she has in months. Matthew knew the basics of what happened with Parker, but he never protested. He simply took the money Parker gave her and handed Miranda pills in return. Matthew isn't her boyfriend, the way she's tried to tell herself. He's not even really a friend.

He's her dealer. That's the plain truth of it.

Stiffening her spine, Miranda makes herself spell everything out, literally and figuratively. **If I get out of this alive, then I'm done. I don't want to see you.**

After she hits the send key, she feels lighter. Even her head feels better. As she deletes Matthew from her contacts and blocks him on everything, she tunes into Cole's whispers to Grace.

"Who knows what's really in immunizations? Look at all those kids with autism. That can't be a coincidence."

Javier lifts his arm from his face and pushes himself up on his elbows. "Do you really believe that? In Mexico, babies die because they didn't get no immunizations."

"You think Americans are really any better off?" Cole retorts. "It's just not as obvious how bad things are here. Corporations like Pfizer and Monsanto are the ones actually running this country. Politicians take their millions and look the other way while they poison everything: our food, our air, our water." His stormy gray gaze goes from one person to the next. "People need to wake up and open their eyes."

"And what would they see?" Miranda asks.

"That people are dying." A muscle flickers in Cole's jaw. "Six months ago, my dad died because he ate a hamburger."

Amina had started fiddling with the computer. Now she looks over, her eyes wide. "A hamburger? Did he choke or something?"

"No. The meat was contaminated with E. coli. None of the antibiotics worked, because the government lets factory farms use them to fatten up animals, and all the bacteria have gotten resistant. My dad died just so chickens and cows can grow a little bit faster."

Grace gives Cole's hand a squeeze, but he doesn't seem to register it.

"My brothers were deployed when both my parents died, but after they got discharged they helped me see the truth. Which is that the people in charge don't want us to know what's really going on. But pretty soon, the government will dissolve, and FEMA's going to start running things. And if you don't like that idea, they've already got over eight hundred camps ready to send you to. They've even got boxcars for moving people, just like the Nazis did."

"Okay," Miranda says slowly. "So there's this massive conspiracy. And no one knows about it or talks about it."

"Right." Cole nods. "That's how conspiracies work."

"So how do you know about it?"

"My brothers told me. But you can see videos of FEMA camps on YouTube."

Cole clearly believes what he's saying, but Miranda sees the flaw in his argument. "How come if the government's so evil and clever, it hasn't managed to pull the videos from YouTube?"

He raises his chin. "Maybe they would rather leave them up so that they can monitor who watches them. So they can build cases against us to say that we're crazy and paranoid."

Or maybe he really is crazy and paranoid. But Cole has lost both his parents. No wonder he's angry. No wonder he sees conspiracies.

"You think this government is corrupt?" Javier takes

his feet off the desk drawer and sits up. "You should try living in Mexico. If you pay enough in bribes, no one can touch you."

Cole doesn't appear to be listening. Instead he points at Javier's back. Miranda follows his finger. Javier's shirt has ridden up. Tucked into the back of his pants is a—

"You've got a gun!" Miranda exclaims.

Javier shakes his head. "I don't."

"Don't lie!" Cole says.

Pulling it out of his waistband, Javier holds it loosely, pointing down at the floor. "It's not a gun, dude. It's a toy. I took off the orange tip. It only shoots BBs. Not bullets."

"Let me see it." Cole holds out his hand and Javier gives it to him. He hefts it, then holds it in front of him and closes one eye as he aims past them.

Even though she knows it's fake, to Miranda the gun still *looks* real, heavy, and serious. "What's the point of having a gun that isn't real?" Miranda asks. Everyone has heard about kids gunned down by cops because they were waving around fake guns.

"Protection."

"From what?"

"Where I live, a lot of Mexican guys my age are in a gang. You can get killed for being in the wrong gang. Three months ago, my friend got shot just because he was an Eighteenth Streeter and he ran into some Paso Robles Boyz. And this is what happened last time I said I didn't belong to no gang." Javier uses his hands to part his thick black hair, revealing a two-inch-long scar. "So if things go bad again"—he takes the gun back from Cole and returns it to his waistband—"this could help change their mind."

"Or it might just make them shoot you with their own, *real* gun," Cole says.

"Why don't you go to the police?" Miranda asks.

"The police?" Javier seems genuinely puzzled. "What are they gonna do?"

"Protect you?"

"The police are there for other people. People like you. White people. People who were born here." Amina looks up from the computer and the two of them exchange glances. "People like me? Beaners who aren't legal? About all they want to do to people like me is deport us."

"Look—we're on TV." Amina points at the computer's screen. "At least, the mall is."

Miranda moves closer, eager for a window into the outside world.

I BELIEVE SHE IS SAYING

5:19 P.M.

EVERYONE CROWDS AROUND THE MONITOR. The computer shows a live feed from KGW with the sound turned off. On the screen, a blond reporter's mouth moves as she gestures with her free hand. Occasionally the picture freezes or pixelates. Miranda squints to read the closed captioning that runs across the bottom of the screen.

". . . hostages pressed up against the windows, presumably to serve as human shields. This is heartbreaking. One girl of about twelve is mouthing, I believe she is saying, 'Help me.'"

The image changes to the exit doors of the mall, the ones Miranda discovered were locked. At least a dozen people are pressed up against the glass doors, with their hands bound in front of them. Many of them are moving their mouths, desperately trying to communicate. If they don't survive, will anyone know what they were trying to say?

"The hostage dressed in a Santa costume is just a sad

reminder that this tragedy is taking place at Christmastime, a season that is supposed to be about peace on earth and goodwill toward men."

The camera cuts back to the reporter, who is now standing with a high school–aged girl. Her long dark hair is shaved on one side.

"I'm with Jackie, who was in the food court at Fairgate Mall when the shooting broke out."

The camera zooms in on her wide-eyed face. "I was standing there, I was just about to pay for a slice of pizza, and I heard gunfire. People were running and trying to hide. I ended up with a bunch of people behind this kiosk that sells remote-control toys. Then we all decided to make a break for it. I kept expecting to be shot, but we weren't."

The camera pulls back to show the reporter nodding. "You were very lucky."

The girl's face crumples. "But I saw people die. It was awful."

The camera pans to show a milling crowd, police setting up barricades well back from the mall, flashing lights cutting through the gathering darkness.

"Police have confirmed that there are as many as eight shooters dressed in black and wearing ski masks. More than a dozen victims have been taken to area hospitals. If you have friends or family at Fairgate Mall, the authorities are advising you to stay away. Police, fire, and ambulance crews need the roads free so they can deal with this ongoing situation. They will be setting up a waiting area at Calvary Baptist about two miles from here, where they will be taking people to be reunited with their families."

Is that where Miranda's dad is right now? Have the authorities made him leave? She hopes not. She hopes he is just a few hundred yards away.

The reporter nods decisively. "The question is: What do these killers want? When we first arrived on the scene, I was given a flash drive by a young man who claimed to have been one of the hostages. He said he was freed on the condition that he hand out these drives to the media. A few minutes later, he was taken in by the police. Barry, do you have any update on that drive?"

The camera cuts to an unsmiling man sitting in the TV studio. "As Jessica said, we do have this flash drive. Its contents are still being analyzed, but it appears to be some sort of manifesto. We are sharing it with law enforcement, but if we get the go-ahead, we will pass it on to our viewers."

"Okay, Barry."

And then a huge blast rocks the storage room.

5:21 p.m.

UNIT 68: We're making entry to Nordstrom.

DISPATCH: Copy.

UNIT 68: The store appears to be empty. The security gate is down. We're gonna—wait, what's that? [sounds of explosion]

DISPATCH: 68. Status!

DISPATCH: 68? Status? 14? 41? 43?

UNIT 14: [static] . . . bomb . . . [static]

DISPATCH: We need ambulance and backup to Nordstrom entry on south side stat!

WAKE UP

THE VIDEO OPENS WITH A SHOT OF AN American flag flying upside down, an official signal of distress.

The camera cuts to a man in a living room with yellow pine–paneled walls and flat tan carpeting. He sits on a brown plaid couch. His face is covered by a black balaclava. His eyes are blue. He is dressed in work boots, jeans, and an ivory-colored T-shirt. His arms are muscled and tan.

The front of the T-shirt portrays a black, bare-branched tree with red roots. It reads THE TREE OF LIBERTY MUST BE REFRESHED FROM TIME TO TIME WITH THE BLOOD OF PATRIOTS AND TYRANTS. —THOMAS JEFFERSON.

The man speaks.

America, it's time to wake up. And we're your alarm clock.

Until today, you've been like babies distracted by shiny toys. You believe what the TV tells you, that you won't be happy until you have new cars and hot french fries and better drugs and bigger TVs. That you won't have a good Christmas unless you buy more stuff that will just fall apart the minute it's unwrapped. And if you don't have the money, you buy it on credit.

As a result, millions of Americans are living a twisted enslavement, while others waste away in prisons, are forced to fight in foreign countries, or exist on the street like animals. So many of us wake in the night worrying we'll lose our homes.

You think you pay for your possessions with money, but you don't. You pay for them with blood. And today we've made that clear.

The world is falling down around you while our public officials—bought and paid for by corporations—act with impunity. Aided by the government you supposedly elect, these corporations have been selling you lies. And you've been buying them. You have let politicians and corporations take your dignity. You've let them grow rich and fat at your expense. But know this: To those who really run this country, you're no more than blades of grass under their feet. They depend on the services of an army of people who are nearly invisible to them. People who pump their gas, take away their garbage, ring up their purchases, install their cable. But if they lost their electricity, their Internet, their access to stores, you'd see how dependent they really are!

We need to return to simpler times, where a man could support his family, where we could trust politicians not to betray us, where we could speak the truth without being ostracized, where companies didn't poison our air and water, where jobs didn't disappear overnight, where people who fought for this country returned home heroes.

Instead, we pamper illegal aliens who take our jobs while our veterans sleep on cardboard in doorways. We let the puppet government dictate every aspect of our lives.

We, the people, don't declare war and we don't make the peace, but we're the ones who fight the battles, the ones who shed our blood and die on foreign soil. And for what? Wars don't help people. They help corporations by keeping the oil flowing. But you've let your young men be sent to war, and then turned away when they come back broken. Well, you can't turn away any longer.

We've shown you what war is truly like. It's death. It's destruction. It's random and cruel. It's broken bodies, broken minds, broken hearts.

It's true that today some will have lost loved ones because of what we've done. But you won't be the first mother to lose a kid, or the first grandparent to lose a grandson or granddaughter. And at least these deaths will have meaning. People will look back and say today was a turning point.

We have been forced to shed blood to make you wake up. To show you that the current system can't be reformed. It can only be blown up.

People of America, rise up. You can start with small acts of defiance, like no longer amassing piles of crap. Or you can go out and sow some destruction of your own.

You can help open more eyes. The only way to truly reform the current system is to shed blood.

It's up to you. Will you be free men? Or socialist wannabe slaves?

And while we've killed, we've also been merciful. There are many more who still live because of our generosity. And if you want them to continue to live, you'll meet our demands.

First, all American troops must be withdrawn from the Middle East.

Second, all veterans must be provided with jobs and housing and financial assistance.

Third, the political system must be reformed so that politicians may no longer accept more than fifty dollars from any individual or corporation.

We know it will take time to accomplish these goals.

As an interim step, you need to do the following.

The message needs to be broadcast nationally. In addition, our friends Eric Piercy, Isaac Mayakovsky, and Joshua Pritchard have to be released from Sheridan federal prison and taken to the Aurora airfield. And you need to provide us with a bus, so that we can take the hostages to the airfield. Once we're there, you will give us a plane and a pilot, at which point we will give you half the hostages. And then when the plane lands, we will release the remaining hostages from the plane.

And know this. We will not release a single hostage until our demands are met. And we will kill ten hostages for any of us who is killed.

WE TOLD YOU
WHAT WOULD HAPPEN

5:23 P.M.

THE NOISE. THE PRESSURE WAVE THAT pushed the door into him. It has to have been a bomb, Parker thinks. Are the other hostages dead?

Is Miranda?

When his ears clear, he hears the hostages out in the hall screaming and crying. But what's worse is that he also hears men shouting. Not in fear, but excitement. It's the killers. Whooping. Like fans of a winning football team.

So whatever happened was something *they* wanted. Miranda said a SWAT team was coming to kill the bad guys. Parker guesses that the opposite just happened.

Lips is yelling at the hostages. "Settle down and shut up, already!"

"Parker," Moxie cries out from inside the cupboard. "Parker, where are you?" Her voice is muffled, but not enough.

Parker shoves his phone in his pocket. He scuttles forward on hands and knees, repeating "Shh" as loudly as he dares.

"Parker! Parker!"

"I'm coming!" he whisper-shouts. "Just be quiet."

Behind him, the door flies open so hard, it bangs against the wall. He looks over his shoulder. It's Lips. Lips raises his rifle.

Parker goes still inside. This is it. His last second on earth. He doesn't pray. He doesn't plead. He just stares at the round empty eye of the gun.

Lips steps forward and puts the end of the rifle against Parker's temple. The cold circle is just millimeters from his brain. Maybe there won't even be time to register the pain.

But the next thing that happens isn't Lips shooting him but candy boxes falling onto the floor as Moxie scrambles out of the cupboard. Concentrating on not even twitching, Parker watches her out of the corner of one eye. Her hair is stuck to one side of her flushed face, and her red coat is rucked up in the back.

So much for protecting her from what's happening. In another second, she's going to be covered with his brains and blood.

And that's if she's lucky. If she's not lucky, she's going to be dead herself.

She lifts her hand and points straight at Lips. "You," she announces, "are a bad man!" For emphasis, she stamps her foot.

There's no turning back now, Parker realizes. They're both going to die. At least Moxie is on her feet, not cowering on her knees the way he is.

"She's just a little kid," he babbles. "She doesn't know what she's saying."

"Oh, don't give me that. She knows exactly what she's saying." To Parker's surprise, Lips grins. "Little girl, you've got some mouth on you."

Moxie, thankfully, doesn't argue the point. Parker has a feeling it wouldn't take much for her to tip the balance from cute to annoying to dead.

Lips pulls the rifle back a few inches and then uses it to prod Parker's shoulder. "You're not supposed to be back here. Didn't you hear? You messed up. You had one chance to come out and you didn't."

He doesn't recognize Parker. Better that Lips think he just chose not to leave this space than have him learn about the phone, the knife, and the cut zip ties. "I've been hiding back here since the beginning. I just wanted to keep my sister safe."

Without turning his head, Parker looks for the knife. It's lying on the floor just behind Lips, partly hidden by the open door. Can Lips see the remains of the zip ties? Are they on the worktable? Is the top edge of Parker's phone poking from his pocket?

"I don't think that's a good enough excuse," Lips says.

"It's the only one I have."

"Get up and go back out there." Lips prods him again. "We'll see what they want to do with you."

The quicker they leave this room, the less chance that Lips will spot the knife or realize Parker hasn't really been back here the whole time. Parker grabs Moxie's hand.

"He was hiding in the candy store's back room with

his little sister," Lips calls as they walk out into the hall. They stop about twenty-five feet from the gate.

Through the security gate, Wolf's ice-blue eyes regard Parker. With his features obscured by the ski mask, it's hard to know what he's thinking. Parker forces himself to drop his gaze. There can be only one dominant male here, and it's for sure not going to be the one without a gun.

"You." Wolf points at one of the college girls, the one in the Stanford sweatshirt. "Hold his sister."

Parker nudges Moxie to the girl. Moxie tries to tear away, so Stanford grabs both her wrists as she twists and squirms.

"We told you what would happen if we found you." Wolf's voice is calm, and all the more frightening for that. "You had your one chance and you threw it away."

Parker stays quiet. There doesn't seem to be much point in arguing or trying to feign abject apologies. Off to the side, he sees an older lady in the white Van Duyn uniform. Van Duyn must be worried he'll try to save himself by ratting her out for hiding his sister.

"Do you believe this kid?" Wolf points his rifle at Parker's chest while he scans the rest of the hostages. His mouth stretches wide in the approximation of a smile. "He thought he could disobey me. He thought he got to choose what to do. No. You all belong to me now. To us." His eyes fasten back on Parker's. "Get on your knees."

With no place to run, no way to help himself, Parker drops to his knees and prays it will be fast.

"But never let it be said that we aren't merciful." Wolf

lowers his gun a few inches. "It's going to be up to your fellow captives whether you live or die. They're going to beat you for your disobedience, and they are going to do a thorough job. But eventually it's going to be up to them to decide when—or if—to stop."

No one moves.

"Come on, what are you waiting for?" Wolf cries. "If you're against the doors, stay where you are, but the rest of you gather around this boy who thinks he can play with your lives."

People begin to shuffle closer. Parker looks up at their faces, but only a few meet his eyes. Some of them are crying, fresh tears streaking already wet faces. Others are expressionless. The guy who was wounded is in front of Parker. Someone has bandaged his arm with a scarf, the price tag still attached.

"Now you need to show him how big of a mistake he made. Show him how angry you are for him putting all of you at risk. And show me that you really mean it. Make an example of him so I don't have to teach the rest of you a lesson."

After a long pause, the old guy wearing white puffy Velcro-fastened tennies kicks Parker in the ribs. It isn't even really a kick that Velcro gives him. It's more like a push.

Businessman, his face expressionless, pulls his expensive shoe back and kicks Parker in the left hip. Hard. An electric shock zaps down his leg.

Parker grunts and drops to his hands and knees.

"That's a good start," Wolf says. "But it's not enough.

It's not nearly enough." He raises his gun again. "Punish him or you will be punished."

The lady with graying dreads makes a noise like a banshee. She looks like the kind of lady who would bake chocolate-chip cookies for her grandkids, but that was before this nightmare. Even zip tied, Dreads manages to grab Parker's hair in both fists and then slams her knee into his nose. It feels like a cold metal spring opening inside his head. His eyes instantly fill with tears as blood splatters the white linoleum.

Stanford is trying to push Moxie's face into her waist, so that his sister won't have to see this.

Parker tells himself he won't cry out. He won't give Wolf and Lips and Mole the satisfaction.

With their hands zip tied in front of them, people mostly use their feet as weapons. Tennis shoes aren't too bad. Dress shoes, with their hard shells, are much more painful. The lady with the crazy tall heels raises one foot, and Parker braces himself to be skewered by her stiletto, but it barely brushes his waist. While he's still trying to figure out if Heels missed him on purpose, the guy with the gauges kicks his thigh so hard, Parker topples. Gauges's second kick just misses him.

Trying to make himself as small as possible, he curls into a ball, his forehead tight against his knees, his fingers cupping the back of his neck. This still leaves a lot of surface area.

His plan to stay silent is quickly abandoned. Grunts are forced from his mouth with every blow. His mouth fills with hot, salty blood. A solid kick connects with the back of his head. He imagines he can feel his brain bouncing off his skull.

Finally, Heels yells, "No. Stop! We have to stop! He's not the enemy. And we're not killers. We're not like them."

Parker uncurls his head.

And then Businessman kicks him in the chin.

5:23 p.m.

UNIT 45: We have to assume that 68 and the others are no longer able to assist. I'll take command until SWAT is on-site. Until then I want two cars at every exit to check for injured, and to check for people who might be armed.

DISPATCH: Copy that. I've got press and family members staging at Calvary Baptist, which is about two miles from the mall. We have requested mutual aid from all local law enforcement. Tigard, Beaverton, Gresham, and Oregon City are sending additional officers. I've got about fifteen Salem officers coming up, and another twenty officers coming down from Vancouver.

UNIT 45: All cars coming in, have them set up a perimeter around the entire mall.

DISPATCH: Copy.

UNIT 10: Do I have permission to take people in cars? I've got a bunch of people shot and no ambulances.

UNIT 45: Do it. Just tell all the hospitals we got people coming in.

DISPATCH: Copy.

UNIT 22: We've got two victims in the back of a squad on the west side of the mall. We'll take them in.

UNIT 84: I have three parties shot over on the east side. One guy's been shot in the neck. Taking them in.

UNIT 45: Officers on foot, be careful, as we've got squads leaving with victims. Dispatch, what's the status on SWAT and the Crisis Negotiation Team?

DISPATCH: They should be on-site in the next few minutes.

UNIT 45: Is the FBI in the loop yet? We may need to get them to activate the Hostage Rescue Team out of Quantico.

DISPATCH: Someone's in touch with the FBI on the fire channel.

UNIT 45: Tell everyone to come into the south parking lot. We'll give them cover.

DISPATCH: 10-4. They have been advised.

SLOWLY, SLOWLY

5:23 P.M.

THE EXPLOSION WAS SO POWERFUL THAT it rattled the cage of Miranda's ribs.

Grace cried out, and Cole pulled her to him. "That wasn't any flash bang," he whispered to them over her shoulder. "That was a bomb." His mouth twisted. "I can't believe they did that."

"One of them exploded his vest?" Javier asked.

Cole shook his head. "I think they set a booby trap for the cops."

A scream came from the other side of one of their walls. "Parker!" It was a little girl. Panicked. And very close. "Parker! Parker!"

Miranda braced herself for the sound of shots. But all she heard was the faint murmur of two men's voices.

Now Miranda's phone vibrates. She pulls it out with a shaking hand. It's a text from her dad.

The cops think a bomb took out the cops who were coming in. Pulling back & reevaluating.

How long until they come? she texts back.

It takes him so long to respond that Miranda already knows the answer before she reads it.

May be long time. Are you sure no way out?

She texts back, **We'll try to think of something.** She can't stay penned up here any longer, shaking from withdrawal, the seconds crawling by.

Be careful. I love you.

Love you too. Tears burn her eyes. Saying good-bye to people is already horrible, but having to say it over and over is worse.

Everyone but Grace—who is still sniffling into Cole's shoulder—is watching her. "My dad says that explosion was a bomb. It took out the cops who were trying to save us."

Amina looks at the computer. "The reporter is also saying it was a bomb."

Miranda's whisper is light as air. "He said that it might be a long time before the cops can come for us."

Grace lifts her head, her eyes shining with tears. "I can't take this. Waiting to die."

"The longer we stay here," Javier says, "the better the chance they'll find us."

Miranda tries to imagine spending hours and hours here. Days.

"What if we tried that back corridor again?" She points. "We haven't heard any shots for a long time."

"I don't know." Grace finds an edge of her blouse that isn't bloodstained and wipes her eyes. "What if it's not safe?"

"And this is?" Amina says flatly.

"Too bad that back door don't have a peephole," Javier says.

A peephole would only show something directly in front of the door. They need to know if there's still someone in the corridor. But if one of them pokes their head out to discover the answer, they could die.

But what if . . . ? Miranda gets to her feet and starts looking through the top drawer of the desk. There! The ruler she remembered seeing earlier. And a roll of tape. Holding her phone against one end of the eighteen-inch-long ruler, she starts wrapping tape around both.

"What are you doing?" Cole asks.

"Sticking a phone out that door is a lot safer than sticking out your head. I can put it in video mode and then check out the back corridor."

Amina looks up, thinking. "To the right, it just ends. I'm pretty sure at Eternity Day Spa."

Miranda pictures it in her head. "And that's off the hall where they're holding the hostages."

"Right." Amina points in the other direction. "The other way goes about fifty feet, but then it branches."

"Where do the branches go?" Grace asks.

"One goes to the mall. The other goes to tenant storage." Amina traces an imaginary path in the air. "But I'm pretty sure that one also goes to an emergency exit. But we won't be able to see it from here."

"If we can leave, do you think you can walk?" Miranda asks Javier.

Instead of answering, he slowly pushes himself to his feet. He takes one step, then another.

"I can do it," he whispers. "Thanks to you guys. Let's go. Let's get out of here."

As they move to the door, Grace looks at Amina. "Maybe you should take off your scarf thing."

"What?" Amina narrows her eyes. "Why?"

"Because it makes you stand out. And maybe these people don't like Muslims."

"I won't deny my faith. Besides, I don't think it matters. I'm pretty sure they want to kill all of us."

As they leave the storeroom, Grace spots a broom in the corner. She spins off the head and gives the handle a few experimental swings before hefting it over one shoulder. Cole has the scissors. Javier holds his BB gun. Amina has the three-hole punch. Miranda carries her phone taped to the ruler.

They don't have to move the bookcase nearly as far as before, but somehow it's harder. Miranda thinks it must be because they're starting to face the truth of what they're about to do.

As they leave, Miranda looks back at the empty storeroom: the strewn clothes, the floor splashed with drying splotches of Javier's blood. It looks surreal. Like a camera crew might step out and reveal it's all a crazy new reality show.

If only.

Miranda walks to the emergency exit and puts her ear against it. Nothing. She closes her eyes to concentrate.

The sound of a tiny bell makes her jump, even though

it's behind her. Amina has opened the cash register. Setting down the three-hole punch, she grabs a pair of long socks from a nearby display, pulls one free, and begins filling it with fistfuls of coins. Miranda doesn't understand, but then Amina raises the filled sock and swings it through the air at head level. Miranda imagines how satisfying it would feel to hit one of the killers, to break his jaw, smash his nose, crush his cheek.

"Can you make me one?" she whispers to Amina before turning back to the door. She puts her phone in video mode, then holds her breath and eases the door open just far enough to slide out the phone taped to the ruler. She tries to move it in different angles as well as up and down, and then she slips it back in, flips it so that it's facing the other side, and sticks it out again. Even though she hears nothing, it's a relief to bring the phone inside and close the door.

Everyone crowds around as she plays back the silent video. It's oddly comforting to be surrounded by the warmth and smells of the others.

The body Amina saw is still there, but there's no sign of anyone else. It's just an empty corridor with scuffed ivory-colored walls, interspersed with plain brown doors. As Amina said, it dead-ends to their right. On their left, it stretches on farther than the phone can see.

"It *looks* safe," Grace finally says.

"What if we realize it's a mistake and need to get back in?" Miranda starts to undo the tape. "That door will lock behind us."

"I've got a key." Amina pats her pocket.

"But what if we get split up?" Javier says.

"We could put something inside to keep the lock from clicking in," Miranda says. "Like gum."

"That's too squishy." Cole has been toying with a cap from near the register and now tries it on. "Maybe paper."

"But if we do that," Amina points out, "anyone could come in."

Grace shrugs one shoulder. "Who's going to try? Anyone back there must know how these doors work. They won't expect to find one unlocked."

Finally, Cole pulls the door open an inch, just far enough so that he can stuff the hole where the lock would normally click into place. He uses the folded-up tag from the hat. Then, one by one, they slip outside, with Cole in the lead and Javier in the rear. They keep in a tight line, each with their weapon.

The weight of her coin-filled sock feels good in Miranda's hand. She thinks of the SWAT team. She's seen photos of men in camouflage lined up like they are now. What if there's a booby trap out here, too?

But the only thing in sight is the woman's lifeless body. She lies on her belly, one knee raised and one arm outstretched, as if she's still trying to crawl forward. Without discussion, they come to a stop.

"That *is* Linda," Amina whispers. "Oh my God. *Linda.* We walked in together today."

Linda has red hair with gray roots. Her head is turned to one side. Her blue eyes are open, fixed and still. Her skin looks like wax. Under her hips is a puddle of blood.

As they pick their way around her, Miranda swallows back bile.

Just before the corridor branches to the right, Cole stops. Nervously, he tugs the brim of his new hat with his free hand.

Then slowly, slowly, he peeks around the corner, scissors at the ready. After a long moment, he nods that it's okay. Miranda lets out a breath she didn't even know she was holding. The rest of them join him.

"If we keep going straight, it just leads to the mall," Amina whispers. She points down the new corridor. "I'm pretty sure there's an outside exit. But this place is like a maze. It's been added on to a million times over the years. Things don't fit together in any logical way. The security guards are the only people who really know the layout."

There's no need to discuss which way to go. They creep down the new corridor, carefully turn another corner. And halfway down the new corridor are solid metal double doors set in the lefthand wall, with a red EXIT sign overhead. They are only thirty feet from freedom.

And then Miranda sees it. Another bike lock stretches across the doors, chaining them together.

There's no way out.

EVERYTHING IS UNDER CONTROL

5:23 P.M.

"IT'S TIME," KARL SAYS TO THE MAN NEXT TO him, the driver of their nondescript white van.

They've been monitoring the police channels. Every cop within a hundred miles has converged on Portland, responding to what is clearly a major terrorist attack.

The driver presses down on the accelerator until the van hugs the bumper of the unmarked tractor-trailer. Both he and Karl are dressed in dark coveralls topped with reflective vests. Except for a half-dozen orange traffic cones, the back of their van is empty.

Karl raises the fob in his gloved hand and presses the button.

Instantly, the cab of the eighteen-wheeler ahead of them is filled with a cloud of pepper spray. For the three guards inside, the effect is instantaneous and overwhelming. It's like being kicked in the chest by a donkey. Every inch of exposed skin is now on fire.

As his eyes involuntarily clamp shut, the tractor-trailer's driver manages to pull over to the side of the road. The three guards stumble out of the cab, coughing uncontrollably, mucous streaming from their noses. One of them starts to vomit. Another flees the cloud spilling out of the cab's open doors, blindly running into a tree so hard, he's knocked off his feet. The third presses his hands to his chest as if his heart is going to burst. But the gas is already dissipating.

Parking behind the tractor-trailer, the van's driver puts on his flashers. He and Karl pull on ski masks and jump out of the van. It's no work at all to relieve the guards of their guns, zip tie their hands behind their backs, and order them to walk into the woods that border this quiet stretch of road. The guards stumble off under threat of being shot. Karl has no intention of shooting them, not if he doesn't have to. It's not like the authorities won't look hard for missing money, but when murder is also involved, they will never give up the search.

Karl and the driver set out the orange cones to make it look like everything is under control. They open the back of the van, then take the keys from the ignition of the eighteen-wheeler and open the trailer. A few seconds later, they start moving the buckets of gold from the larger vehicle to the smaller one. They also retrieve a few of the lighter—and less valuable—buckets of silver, stopping once there's no more room in the back of the van.

Fifteen minutes after Karl pressed the button on the fob, they're gone. Without firing a shot. And with twenty-two million in untraceable precious metals.

COME WITH ME

DESPAIR FLATTENS MIRANDA AS SHE looks at the bike lock stretched across the metal doors. The police aren't coming and all the doors are locked. And even though she didn't hear any shots, Parker is probably dead too. Maybe even his sister.

Muttering, "No, no, no," Grace walks past Cole, grabs the chain, and yanks it.

The locked door, the door that is the only thing that stands between them and safety, is halfway down the corridor. Miranda looks to the other end. Just like the hall they came from, it doglegs, so she can't see more than about thirty feet.

"I don't think we can go that way," Javier says from behind her. "That goes toward where the hostages are."

"We're just going to have to go back to where we branched off and try the other way," Miranda says.

"Back into the mall?" Amina shakes her head hard. "If we go out that door, they'll see us."

"But there must be another exit someplace that isn't

locked. We have to try to find one." Miranda won't give up. She can't. She focuses on that and not on how shaky she feels.

"Hold on," Cole whispers. His fingers have been busy unwinding a paper clip, and now he holds it up. He must have taken it from the desk drawer. "I might be able to get the lock open with this."

"You know how to pick the locks?" Javier asks.

"When you grow up on a farm, you learn how to make your own fun." Cole puts one end of the now-straightened paper clip between his teeth and bites down, then bends it. When he takes it out, it's bent at a ninety-degree angle. He pulls another paper clip out of his pocket and quickly unfurls it. "Spread out and keep watch." He makes a series of tiny bends in the second piece of wire. "This is either going to work right away or it's not going to work at all."

Javier stays at the intersection with the corridor they came from. Amina, armed with her coin-filled sock, faces the new corridor. Miranda and Grace stand in between the two, with Miranda closer to Amina.

A few feet from Grace, Cole kneels in front of the lock. He has tucked the scissors into his waistband. He's biting his lip. The ball cap hides most of his face, so Miranda doesn't know if he's worried his paper clip trick isn't going to work or if he's just absorbed by the puzzle.

His left hand is curled around the lock, and his left index finger holds the paper clip with a single bend inside the lock at about four o'clock. With his right hand, he's plunging the bumpier wire in and out of the lock. His head is cocked as if he's trying to hear the tumblers inside the lock falling into place.

A gasp makes her turn.

It's Amina. Miranda can't see what she's staring at. But she hears footsteps.

Amina's eyes go wide. Her face lights up as if she has just beheld a miracle. "Thank God! Ron! Please, please, Ron, help us get out of here."

Behind her, Miranda hears Cole scramble to his feet and then it sounds like he's running. But why?

It's one of the security guards. A mall one, not a plain-clothes one who works for the stores. Miranda's seen him before. He's got blond hair cut military short, and he wears a light-blue shirt and black pants, along with a black utility belt.

"Why, hello, Amina." His right arm is crooked awkwardly behind his back. A tight smile is pasted on his face. He steps forward with his left arm outstretched, and for an absurd moment Miranda thinks he's going to hug Amina.

Instead he loops his arm around her neck. The move turns Amina and yanks her to her tiptoes at the same time. Her sock filled with quarters clunks to the floor. He raises the thing he was hiding behind him and points it not at Amina but at the others. It's a long gun. A black rifle with a curved clip.

It looks just like the guns the killers used.

Miranda's muddled brain tries to make sense of this. Did he take it from one of them? Because the security guards here don't carry guns. These guards are all wannabe cops, but the worst thing they have is pepper spray. Pepper spray, zip-tie handcuffs, plastic gloves, a walkie-talkie. But not some kind of automatic rifle meant for killing as many people as possible.

All this takes only a second. "You guys," he says, "have to come with me. Or she dies." Even though he's holding the rifle with just one hand, it's clear he could comfortably fire it.

Miranda hears footsteps pound away behind her.

Still holding her coin-filled sock, Miranda freezes. She can't just leave Amina. What if he shoots her? Is there some way Miranda can attack him, save Amina, and not get killed herself?

Over the stranglehold of the security guard's forearm, Amina's panicked eyes meet Miranda's. Her hands claw at his muscled arm but don't find purchase.

He points the rifle at Miranda.

She rips her gaze away. Already starting to cry, she turns and runs while Amina croaks her name.

Miranda sprints flat out. And waits for the bullet in her back.

THE LAST THING
THEY'D EXPECT

MIRANDA RACES AROUND THE BEND IN the corridor. Leaving Amina behind. Hot tears run down her face. Will the security guard—who must also be one of the killers—shoot Amina now?

With every step, the coin-filled sock thumps against her lower leg, hard enough to bruise. Her heart is beating so loudly in her ears that it takes her a second to realize the only footsteps she hears are in front of her, not behind.

Ahead of her, Javier is desperately hobbling forward. He can walk, but he can't run. He's only able to take short strides on his bad leg. Grace and Cole have disappeared. They must be around the second bend, maybe already back in Culpeppers.

It's everyone for himself, like her dad said. Or is it? She catches up to Javier, lifts his arm, and puts it over her shoulder. He turns his head, and one corner of his mouth lifts. With her bearing some of his weight, he's able to go faster.

Finally they round the corner and reach Linda's body.

Miranda tries to go one way around it, Javier the other. She loses her balance, and her foot lands in Linda's blood. They keep going, but her shoe slaps wetly. Miranda looks down. She's leaving a trail of footprints. Her stomach twists. Even if they make it back to Culpeppers, the security guard will know exactly where she is. Where all of them are.

"Wait!" she whispers to Javier. She toes off her shoes, making sure not to get blood on her socks.

Each door is marked with a stenciled store name. Still, Miranda is so panicked that she almost misses the door marked CULPEPPERS.

She wrenches on the handle. But the door refuses to open.

No! Grace or Cole must have pulled out the wad of paper keeping the lock from catching.

Javier taps on the door lightly with the knuckle of his index finger. Will they even hear? And if they do, why should they risk opening the door?

Then it moves a couple of inches, revealing one of Cole's gray eyes. The door swings wider. He leans out, grabs Javier, and drags him inside. Miranda darts in after them. Grace quickly closes the door.

Once she's in the store, Miranda drops her coin-filled sock and puts her hands over her wet face. Her shoulders heave as she cries silently. She can't stop thinking about how the killer took Amina. How Amina clawed at his arm. How her eyes met Miranda's. And how Miranda turned and ran away. How all of them ran away.

Finally her tears slow. She wipes her nose on her sleeve.

Javier is leaning against the wall, shaking his head, his mouth tight and turned down at the corners. He's still clutching his useless gun. Grace is trembling so hard, she looks like she might fly apart. Cole paces between two of the shelving units, up and back, up and back.

Parker's probably dead. Amina's been taken. Now there are only four of them. Is this how it will end? Each of them picked off one by one? Which is worse? Miranda wonders. To die first or to be forced to face death by yourself?

She breaks the silence. "You guys left us out there. You left us all alone."

Cole passes a hand over his face. "I'm sorry. All I could think of was to run."

"And we all left Amina." Grace's voice breaks.

"He's gonna kill her," Javier whispers. "Maybe he already has."

Miranda can't take this. Every change is for the worse.

"But we haven't heard any shots. I think they must have pretended they were shooting hostages so they could lure those cops into an ambush. I don't think he's going to kill Amina," Cole says authoritatively. "I'm betting he put her with the rest of the hostages."

Miranda is still trying to figure things out. "That guy who took her—he's a real security guard. For the mall, not one of the stores." She's walked past him a dozen times, always acutely aware of whatever shoplifted items she had hidden on her person. And all those other times, he's seen her, too, although he's never looked at her with suspicion. But today, when his gaze met hers over the top of Amina's head, his eyes were . . . dead.

Javier nods. "I know him too. His name's Skinner. Ron Skinner. He doesn't like me too much. He doesn't like anyone with brown skin."

They absorb this—and what it might mean for dark-skinned Amina—in silence.

"He must be one of them," Grace finally whispers. "One of the killers. He probably knows this place better than anyone. He probably has keys to all the doors." They all look at the door and then back at each other.

Cole closes his eyes and pinches the bridge of his nose before opening them again. "So what now? Should we go out into the mall and try to find another exit? Or should we stay put?"

"But what about Amina?" Miranda protests. She keeps replaying the moment in her head when Amina looked at her and she turned and ran.

"You're right." Cole points at her, nodding in agreement. "That guy knew her. They'll figure out where we are. We have to leave."

"That's not what I meant." Miranda can't change how she just turned tail, but maybe it's not too late to do *something*. "Amina saved all our lives by letting us into her store. She even fed us. We can't just leave her with them."

"Miranda's right." Grace straightens her hunched shoulders. "We have to help her."

Javier nods. "I agree."

"And just how are we supposed to do that?" Cole gestures toward the front of the store. "Maybe you don't remember, but a bunch of cops just got blown up trying to get in here. And they had guns and everything. We've got nothing but a pair of scissors and a sock filled with quarters."

"But it's like you said about Amina." Grace stabs a finger at him. A few minutes ago, she was sobbing in his arms. Now she looks like she wants to punch him. "The killers can't risk shooting at us, or the cops will force their way in."

"You really want to risk all our lives on my guess?" Cole shakes his head.

"But unlike the cops, *we* don't need to get inside the mall," Miranda points out. "We're already here. And since we ran from that guy who took Amina, they probably think we'll just keep on running. But coming back to get her? It'd be the last thing they'd expect."

"Only a crazy person would go back," Cole says.

"Exactly." Javier smiles and hefts his gun. "They don't need to know my gun's fake."

"That won't matter once they shoot you and you can't shoot back," Cole says. "Besides, what can we do that the cops can't?"

"Right now, they aren't doing anything," Miranda says. "So that means it's up to us." All this talk of cops makes her pull her phone from her pocket.

"What are you doing?" Cole asks as she starts typing.

"Telling my dad about the security guard. If the cops

do try to come back in here, they need to know at least one of them is involved."

Cole looks from one face to another. "I still don't think it's a good idea to try to go up against them."

Grace's laugh is bitter. "Do you really think we're going to make it out of here alive? All the exits are locked and they know where we are."

Miranda's skin itches with the need to move, and it's not just because of missing Oxy. "I don't know about you guys, but I can't hide anymore, waiting for it to end. We have to try. Try to get Amina and then try to get out of here."

"I'm not leaving anyone behind," Javier says. "Five of us were here in this room, and five of us are getting out of here."

And at that even Cole nods.

BRUCE MCGILL, INTELLIGENCE OFFICER, PORTLAND POLICE DEPARTMENT'S CRISIS NEGOTIATION TEAM: Have you watched their so-called manifesto?

CASEY HIXON, HOSTAGE NEGOTIATOR, CRISIS NEGOTIATION TEAM: I just did. A lot of echoes there of other far-right groups. Posse Comitatus. The sovereign citizens movement. Timothy McVeigh. The only thing they trust the government to do is lie to them.

MCGILL: And they think they'll inspire a revolt against the government with that ridiculous piece of garbage.

HIXON: See if you can talk one of the local TV stations into broadcasting it. I'd like to use that as a bargaining chip.

MCGILL: What? We can't do that. We don't do that.

HIXON: There's kids in there. And that means I would read *Mein Kampf* from cover to cover on live TV if they'll just send out one child—one child.

MCGILL: Okay, okay. I'll see what I can do. And I've just learned that if our RP really is Ron Skinner, last year he was investigated by the FBI for ties to an alt-right domestic terrorist group.

HIXON: Then why in the hell is he still working as a security guard?

MCGILL: He was investigated but not charged. And we're talking about an unarmed position, in a mall, that pays a dollar above minimum wage. They can't afford to be too picky. They probably liked that he's a vet. He was honorably discharged four years ago. Plus, it's not like Skinner's got an arrest record. Just one DUI that's thirteen years old. He's single and lives in an apartment about three miles from the mall. We're getting a search warrant.

HIXON: Given that history, Skinner has to be more than just a security guard. He's gotta be part of this. He knew exactly what he was doing. He created the exigency by claiming hostages were being killed. And he's the one who told Portland PD to go in through Nordstrom. He led them straight into a trap.

MCGILL: The question is—were any of the hostages really being killed? None of the officers on scene have reported hearing gunshots since they arrived.

HIXON: Skinner knows too much about how we

work. This is going to be tricky. And we don't even know how many gunmen there are.

MCGILL: The sniper reports that he's in position but he can't see anything past the hostages they've got lined up against the glass doors. And we're still waiting on the blueprints.

HIXON: Our best bet is still to contain and negotiate. If we try another tactical incursion, we could lose more of our people to bombs. Plus, I don't want to force these guys' hands. They've already adjusted to thinking of themselves as killers. If we panic them, more civilians could die.

MCGILL: Roger that.

THEY CAN'T SHOOT
ALL OF US

5:43 P.M.

THE KICK JERKS PARKER'S HEAD BACK ON the white tile floor, now smeared with his blood. Tears of pain fill his eyes.

"Parker!" Moxie screams. Stanford has her arms wrapped around his sister's shoulders. It's all she can do to keep Moxie from breaking free.

With both hands, Heels shoves Businessman, the guy who just kicked Parker's chin, in the chest. He staggers back, while she easily keeps her balance, despite her sky-high shoes. Her black bangs are cut in a perfect straight line right above her eyes.

"Stop it!" she hisses, looking from face to face in the circle around Parker. "We can't just keep going along with them. We're not sheep." Her eyes are the color of gas flames. "You know what happens to sheep? They all get slaughtered."

"Parker!" Moxie shrieks again. Her face is wet and red.

The dozen people clustered around him look from his sister to Heels and then back down at Parker again.

Their faces aren't particularly friendly.

Have things gone so far that they can't be stopped? Parker doesn't know. He just knows he doesn't want to die on this floor, curled up like a shrimp. He rolls to his knees and starts to push himself up. He flinches when one of Velcro's hands moves toward him. But instead of hitting him, the older man grabs one of his wrists and helps him to his feet.

Hocking a mouthful of blood onto the floor, Parker fists his hands and takes a fighting stance. At least his wrists aren't bound like the others'. If he can just manage to stay on his feet, he might survive.

But now no one's even looking at him. He follows their gazes.

A security guard steps out of the entrance to Eternity Day Spa. Parker blinks.

A *mall* security guard. Is he coming to save them?

Only he's carrying an automatic rifle in his right hand. And his left grips the shoulder of a girl about Parker's age. Her turquoise headscarf marks her as Muslim. A trickle of blood runs from one of her nostrils. Her face is expressionless, but her huge dark eyes betray her terror.

So this security guard is no one's savior.

Parker tries to put the pieces together. Has the Muslim girl been hiding inside the spa the whole time? And what about the guard? If he's a bad guy, does that mean all the security guards are part of this?

"Ron," Wolf yells from the other side of the gate, "where'd you get that one?"

Ron tows the girl to the gate, with Lips following close behind. "I found some kids in the service corridor. They were trying to get out through the emergency exit. When I grabbed this one, the other four ran off."

The other four? Could one of them be Miranda? Hadn't she told Parker she was hiding with four other people?

"This is America," Lips shouts, and yanks the scarf off the girl's head.

Her hands clap on either side of her head, fingers spread wide, trying to cover her hair the way someone just out of the shower would cover their body if their towel was snatched away.

Heels whispers to the group around Parker, "You guys, we need to make a plan while they're distracted. We have to turn the tables." Her back is to the security gate. Parker is standing across from her, meaning he can see both her and the killers.

"Plan what?" Van Duyn whispers, drawing out the word as if she's not quite agreeing.

"If we work together, we have a chance." Heels's whisper is urgent. "They can't shoot all of us."

"Yes they can." Businessman shakes his head. "Those are semiautomatics. They could kill all of us in twenty seconds."

———

At the gate, Lips balls up the scarf and tosses it to Ron. The security guard lets it drop to the floor and then kicks it. The scarf doesn't go very far, but it's on the other side of the gate, out of reach.

Rather than crying or begging for it back, the girl drops her hands and lifts her chin. Still, tears shine silver on her dark skin.

Wolf focuses on Ron. "Did you find November?"

"No sign of him." He shrugs. "I'm starting to think he turned tail."

Mole says, "No way, dude. He was right there with us. He even took the first shot."

Ron shakes his head. "So what? The rest of us have seen combat. Like most civilians, he can talk a good game. But when the rubber meets the road, they're all candy asses."

"Watch your mouth." Wolf's tone is a whip. "Our brother's no coward."

———

Our brother? Parker looks from Lips to Mole to Wolf. Lips is short and scrawny. But he can see a resemblance between Mole and Wolf even with their features obscured by ski masks. Both of them with pale eyes and tall, rangy builds. So the missing man—November—must be their brother.

Moxie is still crying and flailing. Stanford finally lets her go, and she runs to Parker. She presses her hot, wet face against his belly. He just hopes he's strong enough to push her away if the hostages attack him again.

"Do you seriously think they're going to let us go?" Heels whispers to their group. "If anyone else tries to save us, they'll just kill them, like those poor cops. But there's only four of them and a couple dozen of us."

"With our hands zip tied," the guy in the Blazers gear points out. Blazers adds, "And there could be more that

152

we don't know about. Like that security guard who just popped out of nowhere."

At the gate, Lips says, "The last time I saw November was upstairs."

"Maybe somebody up there jumped him," Mole says. "We need to go look for him."

"I already checked the cams, and I didn't see him on any of them," Ron says. "Not upstairs. Not down. And he's not in the service corridors. I think he took off." When a snippet of music begins to play, he pulls his phone from his pocket with his free hand. He looks down. "From the caller ID, it looks like they might have figured out who I really am."

"Take it," Wolf says. "You know what to say."

Ron pushes a button and lifts the phone to his ear. "Yeah?" Keeping his voice low, he moves farther away.

As he rubs Moxie's shoulders, Parker toggles his attention back and forth between Heels and the killers.

Heels hisses, "Having your hands zip tied didn't stop anyone from beating up this kid. We need to get one of them by himself." She takes a deep breath. "And then we need to get his gun."

Gauges is the first to nod. "She's right." Most of the others follow, but it's clear that a few, like Dreads, are still reserving judgment.

Heels looks around the ring of faces. "Does anyone have a lighter?"

Parker's lips barely move. "I do."

5:48 p.m.

HIXON: This is Sergeant Hixon of the Portland Police Department's Crisis Unit. Is this Ron Skinner? What would you like me to call you?

SKINNER: Nothing. Because I'm not talking to you.

HIXON: Mr. Skinner, I just want to touch base with you. I'm here to listen to you and to try to make sure everybody stays safe.

SKINNER: We've got bombs hidden all over. You want more cops to die? Then send them on in. We've got so many places booby-trapped.

HIXON: They were only trying to prevent the loss of life. They weren't trying to attack you. You told the dispatcher that the people you're holding were being killed.

SKINNER: Sun Tzu said that all war is based on the art of deception. And make no mistake, this is war. America has turned against its own citizens. That's why we have to take our country back. Do you think this mall is just some random target? In the Middle East they blow up mosques. This is America's church. It's where Americans go to worship. And now the whole world is watching.

HIXON: I'm very interested in hearing what you have to say. And I want to thank you guys for keeping the rest of those people in the mall safe while we talk this out. That's going to count for a lot if we can end this now without anyone else getting hurt. Let's see if we can keep things peaceful for now so we can all come out of this safe, okay?

SKINNER: Don't you understand? Nothing about this world is safe anymore.

HIXON: Are you okay? Are you injured? Does anyone need medical attention?

SKINNER: It's the people we're holding that you should be worried about. You need to meet our demands or more of them are going to die.

HIXON: I appreciate you letting me know where you stand. And I just want you to know that, even though some people were shot at the beginning of this thing, we understand that all kinds of unexpected things can happen in a panic situation. Split-second decisions made in the heat of the moment, right? But you've done a good job of keeping things cool since then, and it seems like no one else has been hurt. Is that right?

SKINNER: More or less.

HIXON: Mr. Skinner, how can we resolve this? I

mean, how can we save these children and women and—

SKINNER: You have our manifesto. You know what we want.

HIXON: I'm sure someone is working on all that for you. I'm not directly involved in the details. I'm here for just one reason, and that's to reach a peaceful resolution. But I'm not going to lie to you: getting that plane might be a little tricky. I mean, we should be able to get it, but it might take a little while.

SKINNER: We want that bus here within an hour or someone's going to die. Probably a whole lot of someones.

HIXON: I'll work on getting you that bus, but I need you to do something for me, okay? To show that we're both acting in good faith. You've probably got some kids there who are crying or some people who are injured. It's going to be a hassle to move them from a bus and then to a plane. Why not give us the ones that are hard to manage?

SKINNER: How do you know about them? Do you have eyes on us? You do, don't you? Well then, I'll just shoot one of them and you'll be able to see them die!

HIXON: No, no! That was just an educated guess. We're not spying on you.

SKINNER: You tell everyone they have to leave us alone, unless they want more people to die. If we see any sign that you are spying on us, then their blood will be on your hands!

GO DOWN SWINGING

5:50 P.M.

"SO WHAT ARE YOU PROPOSING THAT WE do?" Cole says. "It's not like we can go back down to that corridor where he took Amina. If things go south, there's no place to hide."

"We go the other way." Grace points. "Amina said it goes out to the mall."

"Then they'll see us." Cole folds his arms across his chest.

"It doesn't end right in the main hall," Javier says. "It opens into one of the side halls, between Claire's and Pottery Barn. And at the intersection of that hall with the main hall there are two kiosks. We could maybe use them for cover."

Miranda scrolls back through her texts with Parker. "My friend Parker told me there's at least two guys outside that metal fence or gate or whatever it is," Miranda says. "And only one inside."

"If we created a distraction, maybe we could get one

of them to come around the corner to investigate." Grace holds out one fist and then grabs it with the other hand. "Then we could ambush him, hold Javier's gun to his head, and use him as a bargaining chip to force them to let Amina go."

"Hold Javier's gun to his head long enough to get his real gun," Miranda adds. She thinks of Parker and his little sister. "And we'll make them let *everyone* go."

"We aren't even sure if he put Amina with the rest of the hostages," Cole says. "And what's to stop the guy from detonating his vest and killing us all?"

"Would you stop nitpicking everything!" Grace whisper-shouts. "What's the point in worrying about what could go wrong? Everything already has. And the reality is that we're probably going to die anyway. The cops aren't going to want to come in, not after that bomb. Who knows how many places are booby-trapped?"

Miranda takes a deep breath. "I say if we're going to die, we might as well go down swinging."

"You're right," Javier says.

Cole looks at Grace. After she nods, he does too.

Miranda says, "As for the suicide vest, we grab the guy's hands first thing. We don't even let him have a chance to push a button or pull a cord or whatever it is you do." She points. "We can use some of those scarves to tie him up and gag him."

"Then we need to practice." Cole takes the broom handle from Grace and holds it like a gun. Even though it's just a round length of wood, in his hands it somehow transforms into an automatic rifle. "Everyone has to know what to do. If we have to take time to think about it, that's too late." He puts the "rifle" in Miranda's hands.

"Okay, this is what I'm going to do." He catches Miranda's eye and says, "Don't worry, I won't hurt you." When she nods, he says, "Point it at me."

She swings the end of the handle in his direction, the wood slick under her trembling palms.

Cole put his hands up chest high, miming fear and surrender. His hands aren't completely flat—the fingers curl over. With his left hand, he suddenly pushes down the barrel of the "rifle" so that it points at the floor. With his right, he mimes quickly punching Miranda twice in the face. His hand is a blur, so fast that she doesn't even have time to flinch as it stops a millimeter from her nose. Then his right hand grabs the end of the broom handle, the part that corresponds with the stock. With both hands, he twists and yanks the "rifle" back and turns it on Miranda.

She raises her hands over her head, not even really playacting anymore. Her heart is beating so hard that she can feel it in her throat.

Cole shakes his head. "Not so high. Remember to keep your hands in front of your face so you're ready to use them. Now you do it. Take the gun away from me."

"Why do I need to?" She steps back, hands still raised. "I thought you were going to be the one to take the rifle away."

"Because we have to plan for all eventualities. Maybe he won't shoot me, but he could definitely use that gun like a club. So all of us need to know how to get it away from him."

They all take turns getting the broomstick rifle away from each other. And then they add ganging up on the person playing attacker, as well as threatening them with Javier's BB gun and tying them up with scarves. These parts they mostly mime, worried about accidentally hurting each other—especially Javier—or making too much noise.

"But when the time comes," Cole says, "we're gonna make lots of noise. We're gonna overload his senses."

5:50 p.m.

DISPATCH: Police, fire, or medical?

DANA TORRES: Um, police.

DISPATCH: What's the nature of your emergency?

TORRES: I just passed mile-marker ninety-four, and something strange is going on. There's a white tractor-trailer next to I-84. Its back doors are open and there's orange cones out. And there were three guys in the middle of the road. They looked like they were tied up.

DISPATCH: Lying in the road? Are they injured?

TORRES: No. They're standing up and moving around, but their arms look like they're handcuffed or something behind their backs. I don't think they're hurt. They were yelling at me to stop, but I didn't know what was going on, so I didn't. I was afraid to. One of them tried to run after my car.

DISPATCH: How long ago was this?

TORRES: About two minutes. I waited until I was sure they couldn't catch up to me before I called. I don't know what was going on, and it didn't seem like a good idea for a lady all by herself to stop out in the middle of nowhere.

NOT RUNNING AWAY

MIRANDA AND THE OTHERS HAVE MADE it to the open alcove that leads to the hall one over from the hall where Parker had been hiding in a workroom. Next to them is a set of stairs going up, closed off with a swinging bar. The stairs lead to the offices upstairs, where the shooting started. Their eyes dart from the stairway to the hall and back again.

But they don't hear anything. In the silence, Javier points at a security camera. What if one of the security guards is on the other side, watching the feed? Grace uses the broom handle to push the camera so it points into a corner. Then Cole tiptoes to where the alcove meets the hall and cautiously looks up and down. Finally, his shoulders relax. He turns back toward them.

"There's an unmarked door on the far side," Cole whispers. "Probably another service corridor. I think we should take it. They can't have locked *all* the doors off *all* the service corridors."

Javier shrugs. "That security guard could have locked every single door without anyone noticing. And even if someone did, who would they tell?"

The answer hangs unspoken in the air: They would have reported it to the very person who had locked the doors.

Grace breaks the silence. "Besides, we're getting Amina back. Not running away."

Cole makes his whisper even quieter. "I'm just thinking about you. What if things go wrong? What if we never get out of here?" He reaches down and takes her hand. "You've been fighting so hard to live. You don't want to throw that away."

She shakes her head. "You, of all people, should know there are no guarantees. And if we don't fight back, then who will?" She squeezes his hand and then releases it, while Miranda and Javier act as if they haven't been listening.

Earlier, Miranda gulped water from her cupped hands in the store's bathroom, but now her throat is as dry as dust. Even in socks, the bottoms of her feet feel slick. This is it. They're really doing this. But it's still better than sitting in the back of Culpeppers, waiting.

They venture out. The hall is littered with discarded shopping bags, Perk Me Up cups, a few shoes, and a giant stuffed bear that must have been meant as a Christmas present. Other than their careful footsteps, it's totally silent. Eerie.

It's night now. Past the doors, the darkness is lit up by flashing lights from a line of cop cars several hundred feet away. Just like the exit Miranda first ran to, the doors here are bike-locked. But she thinks Cole's right, that there must be some doors in the mall that are open, or at least were at one point. People managed to find ways to escape, didn't they? The bad guys only took the people trapped in that first hall. And if one exit is still open, maybe the four of them can find it. She imagines running down the main hall flat out. Running away from the killers, not toward them. Zigzagging and praying not to get shot.

Only that would mean leaving Amina behind. Amina and Parker and Moxie.

By the time they reach the intersection with the main hall, they're all hugging the wall. After miming what she is about to do, Miranda drops to her knees. Ignoring the screen full of texts from people asking if she's okay, she puts her phone on video mode, then slides it along the floor and a few inches out into the hall. Although it seems unlikely the killers will notice a tiny rectangle on the floor fifty yards away, her hand is shaking. She tilts the phone back and forth and then brings it in.

They move farther back, and the other three crowd around her as she replays the video. It shows the empty main hall, which looks like a larger version of the one they are in now. The only difference is that farther down some of the storefront windows are broken, blown out by the bomb.

The video doesn't show the security gate Parker talked about. It must be set back where the side hall narrows. But it does show the most important thing: two killers in profile, facing the hostages. They're dressed all in black, just like the man who came down the escalator, calmly shooting as he went. In fact, the way one of them holds himself makes Miranda think it is the same man.

"There's still only two of them on this side," Grace whispers.

"Now we just need to figure out how to make one of them come down here. And then we jump him." As she says the words, Miranda feels them in her body. She needs to move. To scream and jump and hit something really, really hard.

"But we don't kill him," Cole says. "Or it will make us just as bad as them." His mouth twists.

"No it wouldn't." Grace spits the words. "We'll never be like them." She shakes her head. "I wish we knew for sure that's where they took Amina. And how are we going to get one of them to come down here?"

"Look—we can take care of both birds." Javier's whisper sparks with excitement. He's pointing at the nearer of the two kiosks, the RC Zone. Miranda has walked by it dozens of times. The guys who work there are always demo-ing toys, hoping to snag some kid who will bug a parent for an impulse purchase.

"Even if we hide behind that, I don't think the angle's right to let us see if Amina's with the other hostages," Miranda whispers.

"That's not what I mean. Look at what they sell." Javier nods at her. "You gave me the idea with your phone."

Cole gets it first. "Great idea, dude!"

"What?" Grace looks just as lost as Miranda.

Cole makes a driving motion with his hands. "We start recording video on one of our phones. Then we put it in a remote-control car and drive it down there!"

IF YOU'RE GOING TO LIE

5:53 P.M.

PARKER'S NOT THE ONLY ONE WITH A lighter. Blazers also has one.

"I'm going to create a distraction," Heels whispers. "And when I do, you guys go into different stores. In the back, pile up paper bags, boxes, receipt paper—anything that will burn—and light it on fire. One of the two on this side of the gate will have to come check it out. And then the rest of us will attack him. Throw things at him, jump him, get his gun."

"But what about the other two guys?" Dreads asks. "They're out of our reach, but they can still shoot us. What are we supposed to do about them?"

Heels's expression doesn't change, but in her voice Parker hears a shrug. "Once we get one of the guns on this side of the gate, I don't think that's going to matter."

———

At the security gate, Ron is saying, "Have you told K-Kilo about how we can't find November?"

"Not yet," Wolf says. "He knows we were looking for him."

"He won't like that," Ron says.

Parker figures Kilo must be their leader, who's off-site.

Wolf throws his shoulders back. "Let me remind you that Kilo put me in charge of this operation." He turns his attention to the Muslim girl. "You. Where were you hiding?"

She presses her lips together and doesn't answer.

————

Businessman's whisper is dismissive. "Do you even know how to shoot an assault rifle?"

"Actually, I do," Heels says matter-of-factly. "Anybody else?"

After a pause, Dreads says, "I shot one once at a range," and Velcro says, "I was in the army for thirty years."

"Then the three of us will rush him. We'll wait until he's inside the store, so the rest can't see what's happening."

————

Ron says, "Haven't you seen her before? Amina works at Culpeppers."

"Is that where your little friends are?" Wolf asks.

There's a beat before she answers. "No. We were hiding someplace else. In a different store."

Wolf's laugh is more like a grunt. "If you're going to lie, you need to do a better job than that."

————

Stanford whispers, "My sister's one of the people up against the doors. If the killers start shooting, they'll be the first to die. They'll be sitting ducks."

"Not if we yell at them to start moving and not stop," Heels says. "It's harder to hit a moving target. And the smoke should make it even harder. Yelling's good anyway. We want as much noise and confusion as possible."

Parker remembers something he saw on the news some months ago. "Last summer the news said if you found a baby locked in a hot car, you could break the glass if you hit the bottom corner with something hard and narrow, like a screwdriver."

"But we don't have a screwdriver," Dreads whispers.

"There's a knife on the floor of Van Duyn's work-room."

"The tip would probably just break," Heels says. "But the handle end—that might work."

―――――

Wolf says to Amina, "So they all just ran off and left you. Where did they go?"

She lifts her chin, and her voice carries. "I don't know. *Inshallah*, they escaped."

Wolf leans closer to her. "And did you see anyone else back in the service corridors?"

"Only Linda from Pottery Barn." Amina's voice breaks. "And she's dead."

―――――

"Start more than one fire if you can," Heels whispers. "We want lots of smoke. We want sprinklers going off. Maybe a fire alarm if they're still operating. The more confusion the better. And then when one of them checks it out, we go for him."

In his mind's eye, Parker pictures the roll of white

wrapping paper in the Van Duyn workroom, the stacks of paper candy cups and boxes. He can start the fire right on the worktable, which will put it even closer to the sprinkler.

"I'll take Van Duyn. But someone has to watch my sister. Has to keep her safe."

———

Wolf speaks into the mic on his shoulder. "Kilo, have they given you an ETA for the prisoner release?"

He waits, but there's no answer.

"Come in, Kilo, come in." Wolf makes his voice louder with each repetition, as if the mic will work better if he projects more. "Kilo, do you copy?"

Ron slices his hand through the air. "First your brother, now Kilo. I don't like this!"

———

"No one's safe," Stanford whispers. "But I'll try." She holds out her arms. "Come here, honey."

"No!" Moxie throws her arms around Parker's waist.

"Shh!" Parker tucks one hand under her chin and raises her face so that her swollen eyes look into his. Greedily, he inhales the sweet scent of her shampoo. "Stay with her, Moxie. I need to help stop the bad guys."

"But *they're* the bad guys," she insists. "They're the ones who hurt you." At least she's still keeping her voice down.

"They only did that because those men made them. Those masked men are the real bad guys, and we have to stop them. Don't you want to get out of here, Moxie?" His whisper falters and breaks. "Don't you want to see Mom and Dad again?" Parker's real life—his parents, his wrestling team, his friends, his school—seems like a dream. In reality, he has always been here, the tastes of coppery blood and bitter fear coating his tongue, his sister desperately clinging to him.

"Yes." Her soft voice nearly kills him.

"Then let me do this, Mox. So we can go home."

Her arms finally loosen.

EVERY RATTLE
AND CLICK

MIRANDA IMAGINES THE TOY CAR, WITH a phone inside, zipping down the corridor far enough to film the hostages, and then coming back. With one of the killers in hot pursuit.

"But what if Amina's not there?" she says. "We won't know until we watch the video." An idea bubbles up. "Does anyone have FaceTime or Skype on their phone? Because if we connected two phones, then we could use one phone to see what the other one sees. That way, it would be like we were actually *in* the car. And we won't have to actually be able to see the car to drive it."

It turns out everyone but Javier has one of the apps. And that when it comes down to it, no one really wants to be the one to risk losing their phone.

Eventually Grace volunteers her phone for the driver's seat. "But what if they just shoot it?"

"It's the same thing I said before," Cole says. "If they start shooting, the cops are going to think everyone must be dying. And then they'll storm in no matter what. That's why they didn't shoot Amina or Miranda's friend. Right now it's a hostage situation. They have demands and they want them met. They won't want to screw that up just to shoot a toy car."

"But what if my phone falls out?" She clutches it to her chest.

"We'll put it in lengthwise so it's more stable," Cole reassures her. "And that way it's less likely to hit the bottom of the gate if I have to go under it to make sure Amina's really there."

"If *you* have to go under it?" Javier echoes. "The remote-control car is my idea. I should drive it. I've played *Grand Theft Auto* a million times."

Cole holds up a cautioning finger. "Before anyone does anything, someone has to get the car. And that means running across that open space as fast as possible and then coming back. And whoever risks doing that should get to drive the car."

Javier looks down at his bandaged leg, then presses his lips together and nods. Miranda and Grace don't argue with Cole's plan.

Before he tries to retrieve the car, Miranda again lies belly down on the floor and slips out her phone, tilting it until she can see the two men with guns. They're both still facing toward the hostages. One of them appears to be talking.

At her nod, Cole darts across. It's less than twenty feet, but it feels like miles. Miranda swallows back bile as she watches the killers and listens for Cole. She can't see behind the kiosk, but every rattle and click makes her wince. Still, the killers don't turn. It feels like forever until her peripheral vision catches Cole peeping around the corner of the cart, but it's probably under a minute. She nods again to let him know that it's okay. Just after he darts back across, one of the men glances up the hall, but his body language shows no sign of alarm.

Miranda pulls her phone in and then exhales shakily.

Cole is carrying a controller and a ten-inch-long white Jeep with an open top. Grace tries to put her phone sideways on the seat. It's tight, but it fits.

Grace takes it back out and connects with Cole on FaceTime. Now his screen shows what her phone can see, with just a small inset square displaying what his phone is viewing. And hers is the same, only in reverse. When Grace fits her phone back in the car, Cole's phone shows her thumb as well as the front of the Jeep's hood.

They have created a mobile surveillance camera.

It's time. Cole sets his phone on top of a display case showing a map of the mall. After tugging on the brim of his ball cap, he picks up the controller.

INFINITESIMAL

6:01 P.M.

MIRANDA USES HER PHONE ONE MORE time to check the hall. The gunmen are still facing the hostages. She nods at Grace, who reaches out one hand just long enough to set the toy Jeep on the floor, tight against the wall. Then she and Miranda join Javier and Cole, all of them staring down at the tiny image on the phone.

From out in the hall, the Jeep makes a high-pitched whine as Cole begins to pilot it, zooming past shopping bags and potted plants, benches, and a freestanding display ad for Hickory Farms.

Seeing things from the Jeep's nearly ground-level point of view makes Miranda feel queasy. Their plan suddenly seems ridiculous. The chances that in a few minutes she will be tying up one of the killers with the scarves stuffed in her pockets are infinitesimal.

To distract herself, she focuses on Cole's intent face. He reminds Miranda of every guy she's ever seen play a video game. It's clear that what he sees on the screen is as real to him as looking down the hall would be.

The Jeep reaches the junction of the corridor and the food court. Cole moves the controller, and the Jeep turns. The gate is ahead of it, with several dozen people penned behind it. Miranda squints and leans closer to the display.

Yes! There's Amina. But her turquoise headscarf is gone.

Standing near her is a guy. His face is bloodied and swollen, almost unrecognizable. But she knows who it is. Parker.

He's still alive. Miranda holds tight to that thought.

Suddenly a man dressed all in black appears to the right of the Jeep. One of the killers. He transfers his rifle to his left hand and with his right reaches behind him and pulls out a gun. A handgun, but it looks weird. Like a pistol, only the barrel is way too long.

NO SAFE PLACE

HEELS TURNS TO BLAZERS. "THE BROTHER'S got the candy store. What store are you taking?"

The guy from AT&T whispers, "There's lots of forms behind our counter. They should burn pretty good."

"Want to take my lighter?" Blazers asks. "I'm not that fast anymore, and you know where all that paper is."

Parker can see the struggle on AT&T's face. Is it better to act, or to not risk drawing any attention to yourself? Then again, whoever is in a store lighting a fire might be out of the not-so-proverbial line of fire. For a moment, Parker wonders if he should take Moxie back into the candy store with him. But Stanford's right: There is no safe place. Not here.

"Okay," AT&T finally whispers. Blazers starts to slide one of his zip-tied hands into his pocket, but Heels gives her head a short, sharp shake. "Give me a couple of minutes. Don't start until I distract them."

Parker wonders what it's going to be. Will she feign illness or pretend to be going crazy? Whatever it is, she risks being slaughtered just like the sheep she originally compared them to.

As he speaks, a high-pitched whine makes everyone turn their heads toward the food court. At first Parker can't place the sound. It's familiar but also terribly out of place. Then something ankle high and moving fast appears on the floor at the edge of the hall.

It's a remote-control car. A white Jeep less than a foot long. It stops about twenty feet from the killers and executes a tight turn. As it comes closer, he can see that in the front seat of the Jeep, a phone lies sideways. Parker squints. Is he really seeing faces on it? Understanding dawns. It must be Miranda and the people she's with.

"Go!" Heels whispers from behind Parker. "This can be our distraction! Go, go, go!"

I DIDN'T KNOW

"WHAT'S THAT?" GRACE WHISPERS.

Cole's eyes don't move from the phone's screen, but his voice betrays his surprise as he turns the Jeep in a tight circle. "He's got a silencer."

Down the hall, the sound is muffled to a loud clap. Then the screen goes dead.

Grace's mouth falls open as she realizes her phone has just been destroyed. "I thought you said they wouldn't shoot."

Cole swears. "I didn't know he had a silencer! We have to get out of here. Go back!"

Out in the hall, one of the killers shouts, "It came from that direction."

Footsteps pound down the hall toward them. All their practice has centered around a curious guy with a long gun and an unwillingness to shoot, not an angry guy with a silenced pistol. They have to get out of this hall before he spots them. Maybe then he might not know where the Jeep came from. Although the kiosk filled with remote-control toys is a pretty good clue.

As they dash for the alcove they just left, Miranda's stockinged feet almost slide out from under her. It's like running in a nightmare. The world narrows to a swath of bright colors, vague smears. Part of her wishes that it was just over. She doesn't care how it ends. Just that it does.

When they reach the end of the hall, Cole puts his finger against his lips and then points. Not at either service door, but at the stairs going up.

Miranda sees the logic. Upstairs, where there are no direct exits, is the last place the killers will look for them. There might even be places to hide.

No matter what, they have to keep moving. Right now, they're all too visible.

They hurry up the stairs, or at least they try to. Miranda feels as if she's moving through quicksand. She attempts to push her fear away, to concentrate on lifting her leaden legs, but it's like she's underwater, weighted down and helpless. Her socks slide on each step. The others are trying to be quiet as they climb, but each footfall echoes.

Cole is in the lead. The muscles in Javier's arms stand out as he pulls himself up with the help of the railing. Behind them, Grace is panting openmouthed, her face contorted with fear. She pumps her arms, the broomstick swinging with each step. As they round the turn in the stairwell, it slams into Miranda's hip. She bites back her cry of pain.

Somewhere below them, footsteps echo. Miranda's heart skips a beat.

How long until it's not beating at all?

STRAIGHT TO
THE SOURCE

6:03 P.M.

PARKER DARTS INTO THE CANDY STORE, his heart a drum in his chest. Once he's behind the counter, he drops to his knees. As he crawls into the workroom, the muffled clap of a gunshot echoes out in the hall.

A startled cry is forced from his mouth. Who did the killers just shoot? Was it Blazers, for handing the lighter to AT&T? Was it AT&T, for trying to light a fire? Could it even be Stanford, the girl holding his sister—or Moxie herself?

Gritting his teeth, Parker forces himself to scuttle into the back room. He can't afford to let terror paralyze him. Should he close the door behind him? What if one of the killers catches sight of the movement? But if he doesn't close it, they might see him. He eases it closed.

As he gets to his feet, Parker grabs the knife off the floor. He reaches back and slips the handle under the waistband of his pants. The small of his back is slick with sweat. He centers the blade so that it's flat against his spine, camouflaged by his polo shirt.

A glass-fronted silver box set into the wall catches his eye. It holds a fire extinguisher. The killers could use it to put out the fire.

He opens the box and then wrestles the metal canister free from its clips. He needs to hide it. Maybe in the cupboards where he put Moxie. Just the glancing thought of her makes his knees go weak. But worry won't keep her any safer, and he can't afford to be distracted.

He forces himself back to the here and now. Maybe he should keep the extinguisher handy. It could be a weapon. Once he gets the fire going, he could wait for one of the killers to open the door, then spray the chemicals straight in his face.

Parker lets out a strangled bark of laughter. If you had told him this morning that by the time the day was over he would be lighting fires and thinking about the best way to damage someone, he would have thought you were crazy.

After he sets down the extinguisher, he spreads his arms wide to gather the gold cardboard boxes and stacks of brown paper candy cups into a pile in the middle of the cool marble worktable. He tears pieces of white wrapping paper off the roll and crumples them. He looks at the ceiling. A metal sprinkler jet is about eight feet above one corner of the table. He scoots the pile so it's right under it.

Out in the hall, it's been relatively quiet. At least there haven't been any more shots.

Parker fumbles the lighter from his pocket. The metal wheel bites into his thumb as he spins it. When the flame appears, he moves too fast. It gutters out.

Taking a deep breath, he tries again, this time cupping his other hand around the orange flicker. He slowly moves it until it starts to lick one of the crumpled balls of wrapping paper. Instead of blazing up, it nibbles delicately on the edge of the paper. The flicker of orange creates a thin curved line of black.

He moves the lighter to one of the gold boxes, holding it under a corner until it catches. Out in the hall, he hears Ron yelling. It's a one-sided conversation, so Parker thinks he must be talking on a phone. He's accusing the person on the other end of lying. Of spying.

The fire is slowly growing from two sides. Parker gently blows on it, and the flames fatten. The black lines turn to crumbling charcoal and silver ash.

Ron's voice gets louder. Parker hears the words "remote-control car."

So they think the Jeep came from the cops. Is that better—or worse—than the truth? Maybe it's better for Miranda and her friends, but it sounds like it's firing up the killers. If they get angry enough, will they start shooting again?

The fire's now about three inches high. Not exactly a conflagration, but it's making a good deal of eye-watering smoke. The gray cloud hangs a few feet above the table, spreading out tendrils that soften the outlines of the room. The smoke scratches his throat. Maybe whatever makes the boxes sparkly gold is toxic. When he coughs, he almost puts out the fire.

Most of the pile is now on fire. But the room doesn't feel any hotter. It's all going so slowly. Parker's supposed to be providing a distraction, but he's not accomplishing much of anything. At this rate the sprinklers will never go off.

He looks up at the one above the table again. Why is he messing around with lighting a fire, when he can go straight to the source?

Tucking the lighter in his pocket, Parker starts to brace his hands on the table to clamber on top. Then he realizes all the paper will be soaked once he triggers the sprinkler. What if he needs it to set another fire in a different store? He piles more boxes and paper candy cups next to the fire extinguisher. Then he climbs on the table, careful not to catch himself on fire. His bruised body protests each movement. He thumbs the wheel, hears it catch, sees the steady orange flame appear. To reach the sprinkler head, he has to stretch his arm above the fire. The air over it is hotter than he thought it would be. The skin on his forearm starts to feel crispy. With his arm stretched full length, he moves the flame back and forth under the sprinkler head. As he does, he braces himself for the water, thinking it will be like taking a cold shower in his clothes.

But when the sprinkler opens, it's like someone has put a fire hose directly above him and turned it on full blast. *Boom!* The water is a shock, pounding so hard, it's like a solid thing. In an instant, the fire is snuffed out.

He steps back, trying to get out of the deluge. But the table is covered with a sheet of water. His foot slips out from under him, and before he can recover, both his feet are in the air and he's falling. When his tailbone meets the marble table, the pain rams all the way up his spine. The sensation is so intense, it's like someone's pressed the pause button on the rest of the world. Parker can't think as he tumbles to the floor. He can't even breathe. He's frozen, trapped in the pain.

But finally, he sucks air in with a gasp. Moving hurts. A lot. But he has to. Someone is bound to investigate soon. The pain lessens a little once he's upright and moving toward the door.

Only now does he wonder if it would have been better to let things build slowly. Now there's really no smoke. No flames. Just water. It's noisy, sure, but will it be enough to attract Ron or Lips? Maybe he should light another fire behind the counter.

Parker flicks his lighter. No response. He shakes water out of the well and tries again.

Nothing. There's no way he's going to be able to light another fire.

NOTHING BUT THE BREATHING

6:04 P.M.

AS THEY ROUND THE CORNER OF THE stairs, Miranda's heart feels like it will beat from her chest. In front of them is a metal door with a narrow vertical window. Stenciled on the door are the words 2ND FLOOR. PROFESSIONAL OFFICES.

Below them, one of the killers yells, "I think it came from over here!" How close is he?

After peeking through the window slit, Cole eases open the door.

With one last burst of speed, Miranda darts through, the others on her heels. Cole closes the door so softly that it doesn't make a sound.

And then they wait to see if they were followed. Miranda covers her mouth with her hand, both to keep her panting breaths from giving them away and to keep herself from screaming. Her nostrils suck air in so hard that they flatten with each inhale. Her pulse is jumping, jumping.

She and Grace are on one side of the door, Javier and

Cole on the other. Grace hefts her broomstick over her shoulder like a baseball bat. Javier clutches his BB gun. Cole holds the scissors next to his head like a crazed slasher.

Miranda tries to ready herself to fight. Where's her sock full of quarters? She doesn't remember dropping it, but she must have. She makes her hands into fists so tight, her nails bite into the flesh of her palms.

She hears nothing. Nothing but the breathing of the others.

Slowly, she starts to shift toward the glass slit in the door. A river of sweat runs down her spine. She shouldn't look. She should stay hidden. But she has to look. She has to know.

The stairs below them are empty. Pressing her face close to the cold glass, she strains to see past the turn of the stairs. There's no one there.

Miranda exhales in a burst. With a little shake of the head, she lets the others know the stairs are empty. Her heart still thudding, she turns the other way.

The short hallway they're in opens up into the second floor, which is shaped like a rectangular doughnut. It's hollow at the center, with the food court below and skylights far above. Offices line the outside edge of the doughnut. The inside edge has a black metal railing.

There are no bodies up here, at least none in sight. But Miranda can see down to the food court, and the carnage there is even worse than it was in her memory. Red smears where people tried to crawl away and bodies where they died trying. And Grace's mom, a broken doll, her hands still stretched above her head from when Grace tried to pull her to safety.

Now it's Grace who has to put her hand across her mouth to stifle her cries.

Somewhere below and ahead of them, one of the killers curses. "All of you stop moving around!" he shouts at the hostages. "Don't make me shoot you!"

Miranda would give anything to be out of here, back at her house, in her bed. She tries to remember how it felt this morning, tries to conjure the feeling of the sheets cool against her legs, the pillow cradling her head, but she can't. She puts her arm around Grace and gently turns her until she's no longer directly facing the sight of her mother's corpse.

Cole puts his finger against his lips, then whispers, "I think I know where we can get a real gun."

Grace takes her hand away from her mouth. They all step closer to Cole, crowding together until their shoulders touch.

"I was up here when the shooting started. I saw this big gun hidden in a planter. I didn't think it was real."

"Where?" Javier's question is as soft as a sigh.

Cole points in the direction of the railing. Spaced along it are three large concrete planters. Each holds a lush plant with foot-long green spade-shaped leaves that contrast with large hooded white flowers. Miranda thinks they're called peace lilies.

"The second one."

She measures the space with her eyes. "If we get down

on our hands and knees and stick close to the wall, I don't think they'll be able to see us."

Cole shakes his head. "Why risk everyone? I'll get it." Before anyone can argue, he drops to all fours and starts crawling. There's less debris up here, but it's still clear people left in a panic. A purse sits in the middle of the floor, not far from scattered papers. Farther on are a wheeled mail cart, a parka, and a box of doughnuts that has spilled half its contents.

When one of the killers speaks, they all freeze. It sounds like he's ahead and below them, somewhere near the food court. "Zulu, return to base. Zulu. Over."

Grace and Miranda exchange a look. *Zulu?*

"G-G-Golf, just give me another minute," another man stutters. His voice sounds closer but behind them. "That toy car has to have come from the cops, even though Romeo said they promised to back off. I gotta find where they are and take care of them." After a pause, he adds, "Over."

"Negative, Zulu. They could be trying to peel us off. Return to base. Now. Over."

Miranda thinks, *What kind of names are Golf and Zulu?* Then it dawns on her that something about these words is familiar.

"Roger that," Zulu finally says, his reluctance plain.

"Any sign of November?" Golf asks. "Over."

"Nicholas? No." Zulu swears. "Do you think the cops got him?"

"I don't know. Just come back. Now. Over."

So is November the same person as Nicholas? Then

Miranda gets it. "Whiskey Tango Foxtrot," she whispers to Javier and Grace. "I think they're using their initials in the military alphabet instead of their real names."

Cole has started moving again. He'll have to get right up next to the railing to get the gun. What if one of the killers looks up and sees him?

Miranda hates having to sit still. To distract herself, she focuses on a black piece of cloth lying a few feet away. It's like a beanie, but with three round holes. On-purpose holes, because they are bound with thread. She gasps when she realizes what it is.

It's a ski mask. The same as the killers are wearing.

Only what happened to the guy who was wearing it?

ANYTHING OTHER
THAN KILLING

6:11 P.M.

COLE IS HALFWAY TO THE PLANTER WHEN they hear footsteps below them on the main floor. Fast and from behind. He flattens himself to the carpet. Miranda and the others shrink back closer to the stairway door. It must be the one called Zulu, coming back.

They can't see him, but they can hear him. It sounds like he's right underneath them. "I don't like this," Zulu says. "I don't like this at all. The cops sneaking around, Nicholas missing. You should've let me keep looking. Maybe I could have found him or figured out where the cops got in."

"Remember what Kilo said," Golf says through Zulu's mic. "That we have to stick together, no matter what."

"Yeah, and where's Karl, Kilo, whatever now? Kicking back at the airfield while we take all the risks. He didn't even answer the last time you tried him."

Golf keeps his tone even. "He said that he was going to be in and out of range."

A third voice chimes in over the mic. "The negotiator promised that the cops were going to keep back. Obviously that was a lie. Things are going south. Nicholas is missing, Karl's not responding, and the cops are trying to spy on us."

"This isn't how it was supposed to go down," says a fourth man on the mic.

As they are speaking, Cole cautiously starts to move again. He's only a few feet away from the planter. And tucked behind the planter is a—Miranda squints—a weird-looking black, bulky vest with a dozen pockets.

A cold finger traces her spine as she realizes that it's a suicide vest, just like the ones the killers are wearing.

"I don't understand how the cops or FBI got close enough to send that remote-control Jeep right up to us like that," Zulu says. "All the nearby exits are locked. We've got clear lines of sight. We should have spotted them right away. But they're obviously here and we don't even know where they are."

"All the more reason we can't have you go running off," Golf says. "We can't afford to lose someone else."

"We need to get out of here," the third man says. "We need that bus and we need it now. I told the negotiator that they had better hurry if they don't want more people to die."

A bus? Is that slang for something? Miranda exchanges puzzled looks with Grace. A bus doesn't sound like the ideal getaway vehicle. Slow, lumbering, huge turning radius. Then Miranda gets it. The one good thing about a bus is that it can hold a lot of people. The killers must be planning on taking at least some of the hostages with them.

Layered under the voices is another noise. Miranda tilts her head, straining to hear. She can't quite place it. It's like someone has left a hose running.

Javier taps her shoulder and then points across the way. On the other side of the second floor, across the mall, an open office door reads MALL SECURITY. Just inside, two uniformed men are sprawled facedown on the carpet, unmoving. One of them is bald except for a half circle of gray hair. Miranda has walked past him a dozen times, carefully looking neither at him nor away.

She had wondered if the coworkers of the security guard who took Amina were in on this thing. The dead men must be the answer. It looks like they were ambushed. If you have to die, is it better to be unaware until the end, and maybe not even then?

Miranda wrenches her gaze back to Cole. She pretends that the right-hand corner of her vision doesn't work. That she can't see the bodies in the food court, the bodies in the security office. That the lack of Oxy hasn't left her shaking and nauseated.

Cole reaches the planter and rises to his knees. One hand pushes aside the leaves, and the other plunges in and then reappears with the rifle. It's a dull black. The butt ends in a flat, elongated rectangle. Miranda guesses that's so you can brace it against your shoulder. In front of the trigger sits the curve of the clip. The rifle looks all business. It's clearly not meant for anything other than killing.

Cole starts to crawl back, but it's hard to both crawl and carry the gun. He looks over at the food court, and after checking out its emptiness he gets to his feet. Pressed close to the wall, he starts walking back to them.

"I still say we need to know where the cops are," Zulu says, his voice rising. "What if they're planning an ambush to get us back for *our* ambush?"

"Let me try to raise Karl again," Golf says. "Kilo, come in. Kilo. Over."

One of the killers moves into Miranda's field of vision. She sucks in her breath. If she can see him, he can see them. All he needs to do is look up and over. And with the jittery way he's moving, turning his masked head from side to side, it seems quite possible that he will also think about the space overhead. They have to get out of sight. Now!

As she, Javier, and Grace creep backward, panic zaps through her. They have no way to warn Cole.

But when he sees them retreat, he drops to his knees. He scuttles forward, pushing the rifle ahead of him.

Miranda scrambles into the nearest office. It's small, with just a desk and three chairs. The others follow. After Cole crawls inside, Grace closes the door before Miranda has time to wonder if the movement will catch the killers' eyes.

What if they were seen? Miranda grabs a narrow white three-ring binder labeled 2017 INVOICES, lays it on its side, and shoves the narrow end under the door until it gets stuck. It's like a doorstop. Now if anyone comes up here and tries the door, they won't be able to shove it open. Cole nods approvingly.

Miranda feels a flush of pride. Then she realizes that if the killers get suspicious, they can just shoot through the door.

"So that's an AK-47?" she whispers as she looks at the gun lying on the carpet next to Cole.

He shrugs one shoulder. "An AR-15."

"What were you doing up here that you saw it?" Grace asks. The strain of the past couple of hours shows in her voice.

"Um, making deliveries. I work for an office-supply company."

Javier nods. "I thought I'd seen you around before."

"I spotted the rifle when I was trying to get out," Cole says. "They must have staged this stuff up here for someone who didn't come. Maybe someone who backed out."

Miranda thinks of the ski mask she saw near the gun. "I don't think this stuff was up here waiting for someone who didn't come. I think someone had it all on and *then* decided to take off. He got rid of it along the way. First the gun, then the suicide vest, then the ski mask."

"You could be right." Cole straightens up. "Hey, maybe I can pretend to be him! The guy who took off. If I put on the vest and the ski mask and then walked up to that gate, I don't think they'd be able to tell me apart from the real guy they're looking for, at least not at first. If I keep my mouth shut, they might not know any better until it's too late." His mouth thins to a line. "And then I'll do what I gotta do."

Javier pulls his brows together, looking worried. "Or they'll just kill you."

Miranda is trying to figure out whether Cole's idea will even work, when Grace says, "Only you won't be pretending if you put on that vest and mask. Because you were wearing them in the first place. You're one of them, aren't you?"

In the stunned silence that follows, she launches herself at Cole. Her hands circle his throat.

"And you're the one who killed my mom!"

YOU HONESTLY BELIEVED

S OAKING WET, CLUTCHING THE FIRE EXTIN-
guisher to his chest, Parker waits for one of
the killers to walk into Van Duyn's workroom.

And waits.

And waits.

Finally he can't stand it anymore. The water is thun-
derously loud as it jets from the sprinkler, but for some reason no one is coming to investigate. Parker edges open
the workroom door, then ducks down behind the front
counter. As he crawls out into the main part of the store,
he nudges the fire extinguisher ahead of him. The little
finger of his left hand looks like it might be broken. His
butt is stiff and painful. His left eye throbs with the beat
of his heart. Every part of his body complains.

Still on his knees, he peeks out the entrance of Van
Duyn. The killers are all clustered at the gate, paying no
attention to the hostages. Most of the hostages sit slumped
on the floor, exhausted by the ordeal. A few are more alert

and anxious, eyes darting, trying to figure out their next move.

"Kilo? Come in, Kilo. Do you copy?" Wolf says. "Over." The strain in his voice tells Parker it's not the first time he's said those words.

When the killers' mics crackle, they all jump. "This is Kilo," a disembodied voice says. "Over."

Across the hall, the back of the AT&T store is starting to fill with thick gray smoke. Parker catches a glimpse of the guy who works there, on his knees behind the counter, feeding the flames a stack of forms a few at a time. Looking at AT&T's fire, Parker wishes he had let his smolder instead of forcing the sprinkler to go off. Even as smoke is starting to roll out of the store's door, though, the killers are still focused on the voice of the man who must be their leader.

"How are things going at the airfield? Have our people gotten there yet?" Wolf asks. "Or the plane? Over."

"The plane?" Kilo echoes. "You honestly believed there would be a plane? Tell me, do you also believe in the Easter Bunny and Santa Claus?"

After a second of shocked silence, the four killers all speak at once, swearing and demanding that he explain what he means.

Kilo's voice cuts in, his calm tone a sharp contrast to that of the others. "Did you really think this whole thing was going to work? That the cops and the FBI were going to let you leave in a bus—a bus!—with a few dozen hostages? And then give you a plane and just let you fly away?"

His laugh is showy, fake. "If so, then you guys are even dumber than I thought. There's no way any of that is going to happen. You're terrorists, even if you're Americans. And the government doesn't negotiate with terrorists."

"Why do you keep saying 'you'?" Mole demands. "We're in this together. If we're terrorists, then *you're* a terrorist."

"Sorry, bro. What you are is a distraction. And what I am is rich. See, I had a little side project, one worth millions in gold. The only problem was how to get away without getting caught. That's why I want to thank you. Because what you've done today? That's tied up every cop and deputy and FBI agent for miles. And since they're all busy with you at the mall, they don't care about little old me."

"Wait a minute," Lips says slowly. "When's the plane coming? I don't get it."

"Idiot!" Ron gives Lips's shoulder a shove. "He double-crossed us."

"But what about the cause?" Wolf asks.

"What about it?" Kilo says. "Nobody cares. Nothing's going to change. Timothy McVeigh blew up the Murrah Federal Building in Oklahoma and killed 168 people. He thought he'd inspire a revolt against the government. All he got was a lethal injection. And how about 9/11? Two freaking buildings collapsed and nearly 3,000 people died. But did anything fundamental change afterward? No."

"Our message will still get out!" Mole insists, but his voice trembles.

"I used to be like you guys," Kilo says. "I thought I

could make people listen. But they're not going to change. They don't want to. They like buying crap. They like mindless TV. They like caring about celebrities. And they don't really care if politicians lie or the army sends poor kids overseas to die. They don't *want* to know how things really work. Just as long as they have their creature comforts." He makes an amused noise. "And you know what? I've realized I'm not that much different."

Wolf shakes his head as if Kilo can see him. "Right now, we're being carried live on every news site and TV station," he insists. "And they're going to broadcast our manifesto. People are paying attention to the cause."

"And once the live feed ends because you've all been killed," Kilo says matter-of-factly, "people will stop watching and go on to the next entertainment."

"Forget you!" Lips says. "We'll tell the cops it was all your idea. You planned the whole thing."

"I'm afraid you're not going to be able to do that, Timmy," Kilo says. "Because we've come to a parting of the ways."

"Yeah!" Wolf says bitterly. "You're abandoning us here."

Kilo answers, "That's not exactly what I mea—"

The last syllable is cut off by a tremendous explosion.

THREE INCHES AWAY

EVERYONE STILLS AS GRACE'S HANDS close on Cole's throat. Miranda looks at the door. Has Grace's shout just given them away?

"Shh, Grace, they'll hear you."

"I don't care who hears me." Grace's eyes glitter with unshed tears, but she doesn't loosen her grip on Cole's neck. "Cole, or whatever the hell his name is—he's the one who shot my mom!"

Cole opens his mouth, but all he manages is a choking sound.

In Miranda's memory, the whole ordeal rearranges itself, like those pictures made of thousands of tiny photos you have to step back to see. It's possible. But it can't be true—can it? Her rib cage is a fist around her heart.

Suddenly the light goes on. "That Nicholas they couldn't find," she says. "It's him. They called him November because of the military alphabet, but it's Nicholas. Nick-*Cole*-Us. Cole."

Cole's gray eyes are bugging out as his face turns a

dusky shade of red. A vein stands out on his forehead. But he doesn't struggle, doesn't even pull on Grace's hands, even though she seems intent on killing him. Instead he stares into her eyes.

Miranda can't watch one more person die right in front of her. She leans close to whisper in Grace's ear.

"Let go, Grace. Come on. Let go." Miranda's fingers pull at the other girl's, but they stay as taut as wires. "This won't solve anything. It won't bring your mom back."

Grace finally releases Cole's neck.

And then she reaches for the rifle.

Oh, hell no. Miranda grabs it up first. After a moment, she jams the muzzle against Cole's chest. She might not want to see him die, but right now, she doesn't mind leaving him with a few bruises. She keeps her finger off the trigger.

Unlike the scenario he made them rehearse, Cole doesn't pretend to be surrendering while really keeping his hands ready to grab the rifle. He doesn't move his hands at all, not even to swipe at the blood trickling down his neck from the red half-moons Grace's nails cut on his throat.

Finally he speaks. Or tries to. "I . . . don't . . . You see, I . . ." he stammers.

"Oh, I see all right," Miranda says. "The reason you knew about this rifle is that it's *your* rifle. And you knew exactly where it was because you're the one who left it there."

Grace sneers. "What happened? Did you shoot my mom and then chicken out? Drop the gun, take off the vest and mask? And then you tried to pretend you were one of us. You tried to pretend that you were human." Her voice breaks on the last word.

Cole doesn't answer. But his pale eyes are full of what Miranda would swear was sorrow.

Javier curses. "Who are you, dude? Are you really one of them?"

"You're their brother, aren't you?" Miranda says. "But you said your brothers were dead." Hadn't he? Or had he just said his brothers *were* in the army as he'd looked toward the food court, and she had misunderstood what the past tense meant?

Cole straightens up as much as he can with the muzzle of a rifle pinning him to the wall. "I didn't lie to you."

"Oh, so it's okay to kill my mom but it's not okay to lie?" Grace scoffs.

"Look, what I told you guys was true. My parents died the way I said. And my two brothers, Gabriel and Zach"— *Golf and Zulu*, Miranda translates in her head—"were in the army. I grew up wanting to be just like them. Only after they were discharged, they couldn't find work. The only jobs they could find were at this cruddy mall where everyone calls them wannabe cops and makes fun of them. But they've opened my eyes. Now I know what's really going on overseas. What's really going on in this country. And we joined a group of other people who felt the same way. This guy Karl, he's in charge. He picked this mall because my brothers and Ron, the guy who took Amina, worked here. And they got another of the guards to join them." Cole sucks in his lips until they disappear.

"Karl said the only way to get America to listen would be to do something so big that no one could ignore it. And it all made sense, I swear it did. But then today . . ." His voice dwindles. He tries again. "Today, after I . . ." Cole looks from Miranda to Javier and finally to Grace. His mouth closes, opens, and closes again.

"What?" Grace bites off the word. "Come on, say the rest of it. 'After I shot your mom.' You do something so awful and then you can't even be man enough to own it, to live with it?"

"I'm—I'm sorry." He blinks, and a tear runs down his face. "As soon as I did, I realized it was all a terrible mistake."

Grace's incredulous smile is like a gash in her face. "It doesn't make it any better that you're sorry. In fact, it makes it worse." She gives her head a short, sharp shake. "Because if you had only thought to be sorry before all this happened, then maybe it wouldn't have. Or at least my mom would still be alive."

Cole's mouth twists. "So what are you supposed to do when you make a mistake? When you make a mistake and there's no way you can take it back, no way you can fix it? Because it's already done. It's already over." His voice is rough with tears. "I tried to save who I could. And then when I met you, I thought I could get us out of here, or at least I could get you out. But I couldn't even do that."

Miranda thinks of how the security guard grabbed Amina. About how Cole left her and Javier behind. She jabs him with the rifle. "You didn't even try, you liar! You led us right into a trap."

"If I'm lying, why did I run when Ron took Amina? Why didn't I help him capture you? All I wanted was to help you find a way to escape. But you wouldn't let me. You *had* to go back for her. You weren't willing to cut your losses."

"Cut our losses?" Grace echoes. "You mean we should have just let Amina die?"

"What's worse? One person dying or five people dying? Besides, I wasn't lying when I said I didn't think they would kill her. Yes, some initial sacrifices had to be made, but after that the plans called for us to hold hostages and use them as bargaining chips." He takes a deep breath. "But I must not know all their plans. Like I didn't know they were going to blow up those cops."

"So you would have stopped them if you knew?" Javier demands.

Cole pauses before his answer, and the pause is answer enough.

Miranda doesn't wait for him to speak. "They were talking about a bus and a plane. What's supposed to happen now?"

"We were asking for a bus so we could take the hostages with us to an airport. And they had to release three of my brothers' friends from prison and take them to the airport too. Once we got on the plane, we were going to release half the hostages. And then we were going to fly someplace—they never told me where—and when we landed safely, then we would let the rest of them go."

"And you really thought that was all going to happen?" Javier's voice is flat.

Cole is silent.

Miranda had been thinking. "Well, right now, we're going to do that stupid plan you came up with. With some slight modifications. We're going to march you down there. You're not going to wear a mask or a vest. And we'll tell them we'll kill you if they don't open everything up. The metal gate, the doors." She pokes him with the barrel of the gun. "And if they don't, well, at least I know how to keep my promises."

"Do you even know how to shoot that thing?" Cole asks.

Miranda shrugs. "If I'm three inches away, I don't think that will matter much."

NOT ANYMORE

LASS SHATTERS. EVEN THOUGH HE'S ON his knees, the pressure wave almost knocks Parker over.

Was it another bomb? A cloud of white smoke has engulfed the killers. And it smells like . . . like . . . like . . . barbecue.

As the smoke begins to dissipate, Parker blinks. There's no Lips. Not anymore. In the spot where he was standing lies a mangled torso clad in the torn remains of the suicide vest. A hand lies on the floor just a few feet ahead of Parker. A hand. Not attached to anything else.

His face contorted in disgust, Ron backs away from Lips's remains.

Over the ringing in his ears left by the bomb, Parker also hears the other hostages screaming in shock and fear. Stanford has pressed Moxie's face into her waist.

Mole swears. "Why did Timmy set off his vest?"

"He didn't," Wolf shouts, tearing at the straps of his own suicide vest. As his rifle clatters to the floor, he tosses the vest in the direction of the food court. It explodes in midair. Frantically following Wolf's example, Mole fumbles with the straps on his own vest. But the next explosion is farther away. It sounds like it came from the open second floor of the mall. Mole manages to get his vest off and pitch it away just before it explodes.

While everyone is still shocked into stillness, a barefoot Heels runs toward Lips's rifle, which landed under a bench. She drops into a baseball slide as she reaches toward it.

But just as her outstretched fingers touch the gun, Ron runs over and puts his foot on it. Bracing his own rifle against his shoulder, he aims at Heels as she desperately tries to scramble back.

No! Parker is already moving. He points the fire extinguisher's hose straight at Ron's face. His thumb depresses the trigger.

With a *whoosh*, a fine pale-yellow powder shoots out of the end of the black hose. The grains are packed so close together they seem almost like a liquid. Ron shouts, then starts to choke and gag. His features are obscured by the powder. Still holding his rifle with his right hand, he tries to pull his shirt over his mouth and nose with his left.

The noxious yellow cloud has begun to envelop Parker, too. As he starts to cough, he forces his hand not to waver. He has to keep the other man from killing Heels. From killing them all.

She pushes herself to her feet and starts to run away. Blindly, Ron depresses the trigger of his rifle. Bullets stitch the floor behind her but don't find any other target.

With a banshee yell, Gauges launches himself at Ron from the side. He grabs the barrel of the rifle and pushes it down, then wrenches it away.

"Everybody freeze!" Wolf yells out from the other side of the gate.

"No, don't!" Heels yells. "Don't do anything he says. It's time to fight back." She reaches into an open shopping bag and lobs something the size of a grapefruit. It slips between the diamond-shaped openings of the security gate and catches Wolf square in the chin. It looks like a round bottle of yellow body lotion. He staggers back, but more in surprise than pain.

Gauges was not one of the people who claimed to have experience with rifles, and it's obvious he has no idea what to do now that he has one. He points it at Ron. But then Ron drops to his knees, gagging and coughing, clearly no longer a threat. Gauges pivots to point the rifle at the killers at the gate. But there are panicking hostages between him and them. He swivels back and forth, undecided.

Even with Ron on his hands and knees, Parker doesn't let up on the fire extinguisher. "I got the knife," he yells at Heels. "It's under my shirt in the back."

She runs up behind him. He feels her peel up the wet cloth, and then her fingers dip under his waistband.

Clutching the knife, she dashes to one of the glass exit doors. She falls to her knees between two of the hostages and starts hammering on the lower corner of the glass with the tip of the wooden handle.

The fire extinguisher starts to sputter. Ron is now curled facedown like a turtle, but Parker doesn't stop spraying. He chances taking another quick look around. Everyone is in motion. Some people are throwing things at Wolf and Mole. Some are running in panicked circles. Some people are trying to hide in stores, behind fixtures, even behind other people.

The fire extinguisher is still making noise, but nothing comes out of the hose. It's empty.

Parker releases the trigger and then looks up. Something is happening on the far side of the gate. More and more hostages are staring in that direction. Wolf and Mole have turned their backs and are looking out at the food court.

Parker follows their gazes. A group of people is heading toward them, cutting around the tables and overturned chairs and the occasional body. In the lead is a guy in a baseball cap. His hands are raised. Behind him is a girl dressed in jeans and a red oversize sweater. She's holding an automatic rifle, and every few steps she prods the guy with it.

It's Miranda. She's alive! A sudden blaze of joy engulfs Parker.

Behind Miranda are—he squints—two more people. One is the busboy from the food court. He's limping, and his leg is bandaged. And behind him is a skinny girl wearing a blouse stained with blood.

"Open this gate," Miranda demands. "Open it up or I'll kill your brother."

"**P**UT DOWN YOUR GUNS AND OPEN THIS gate," Parker hears Miranda repeat. "Right now. Or your brother dies." Her face is pale and calm, almost mask-like, but her voice is raw with emotion.

For emphasis, she prods the guy in the ball cap, hard enough that he stumbles forward. He's tall and rangy, with pale eyes. Just like Mole and Wolf.

"Are you okay, Nicholas?" Mole asks.

"Just do what she says, please." His voice cracks. "She means it."

A movement in the corner of Parker's eye makes him turn. Ron has managed to get to his feet. Now he stumbles away, tears and snot streaming down his yellow-coated face as he coughs and gags, bent almost double. One hand on the wall to guide him, he rounds the corner into the day spa.

Parker follows. He doesn't trust Ron, but his only weapon is out of ammo.

All around them is chaos. The air is filled with the

soapy smell from the fire extinguisher, as well as smoke from the AT&T store, where the sprinklers have still not kicked on. From Van Duyn comes the pounding of falling water.

But there's no longer a need for a distraction, not now that Parker has taken care of Ron, Lips has exploded, and Miranda is ordering around the other killers at gunpoint.

Still carrying the fire extinguisher, Parker enters the day spa. Ahead of him, Ron staggers past the receptionist's desk to the first of a half-dozen black hair-washing sinks. He grabs the edge of the sink with his meaty fists, doubles over, and starts throwing up. Even his vomit is pale yellow. What kind of chemicals are in a fire extinguisher, anyway? Could they kill someone? Still gagging, Ron turns on the faucet and sticks his face under the stream of water.

Past him, Parker's eyes are drawn to a set of tools laid out on a white towel. They remind him of surgical tools in one of those TV medical dramas, but because they are next to a display of colorful nail polishes, he thinks they're probably actually for manicures. He squints. One of the tools appears to be a small purple cordless drill. He moves closer. It *is* a drill, complete with a bit that comes to a tiny, spade-like tip.

He looks out into the main hall. Heels is on her knees. She's freed her hands and is still using the butt end of the knife to hammer at the glass door. Even though she's hitting it so hard that she's risking stabbing herself in the chest with every backswing, it's refusing to crack.

Parker snatches up the manicure drill and runs to the

spa's entrance. He realizes he has no idea what Heels's name is. "Hey! Hey!" he yells until she looks up. "Try this!" Leaning down, he slides it across the floor to her. After she stops it with an outreached hand, her face lights up.

When Parker turns back, the water is still running in the hair-washing sink, but Ron is gone.

No! He spins in a circle, his breathing speeding up. Where did he go?

There! Out in the main hall, he spies Ron's black utility belt and blue polyester shirt, now splotched with water and yellow chemicals. Even though the guard no longer has a rifle, frightened hostages are scattering in front of him. Parker runs after him.

At the far end of the hall, Wolf and his brother have their hands in the air while Mole unlocks the security gate, all under the watchful eyes of Miranda and the busboy, who has somehow acquired a pistol.

Parker is about twenty feet away when Ron grabs someone from behind. It's Amina, that girl from Culpeppers. His right arm is tight around her neck. When he raises his other hand, something catches the light. It's a metal nail file. Because he's behind them, Parker can't see exactly what he does next, but it looks like he's pressed it against Amina's throat. At least that's where Parker hopes it is. *Against* her throat, not *in* it. And he also hopes that Ron is thinking about the future. About how a live Amina could be used as a bargaining chip.

With shaking hands, Gauges raises the assault rifle and points it in the general direction of its original owner.

But any bullet that hits Ron will probably go through

Amina first. And that's if Gauges has good aim. If he doesn't, he could take out any of the dozen people near Amina and Ron. Including Parker.

"No!" Parker yells. "Don't shoot! It's not safe."

From behind him comes a shattering sound that's almost musical. *What the—?* He turns. The glass door has finally broken. Heels snatches her hand out of the way, but it's safety glass, a rain of blunt-edged fragments. It crinkles and pops as the glass gives way higher and higher up. Pulling her sweater sleeve over her hand, Heels starts knocking out the remaining glass from the bottom square of the door.

Ron has also been distracted. Parker seizes his chance. He runs toward the bigger man. Holding the end of the empty metal fire extinguisher in both hands, he swings it like a club at Ron's head, on the opposite side of where Amina is. She's short enough that she is tucked in the other man's armpit.

Ron raises his left forearm, blocking the blow. It lands with a meaty smack. The nail file flies out of Ron's hand— but the fire extinguisher also slips from Parker's grasp. It lands on the floor about ten feet behind the security guard.

Ron swings a left roundhouse at his head. Parker ducks. The blow glances off the top of his head, but is still hard enough that it tugs his hair.

Amina reaches back to claw at Ron's face. Her finger-nails leave red furrows, and he lets out a yell. She squirms out of his grasp and runs away, leaving Ron and Parker facing off against each other.

The security guard stands angled, his hands loose fists

held close to his face as he bobs and weaves. It's clear that he has been in fights before. Ron is taller, so he has more reach. And Parker might be a champion wrestler, but that's on a mat with rules and a referee and someone in his weight class. With the fire extinguisher now out of reach, he's lost the only advantage he had.

In a split second, Parker runs through his options. A double-leg takedown? But then what happens once they are on the floor? Or should he change levels, get up under the security guard, lift him, and then try to slam him into the floor, knocking him out? But Ron probably has fifty pounds on him.

Then it comes to Parker. A choke from behind. Like all wrestlers, Parker's played around with mixed-martial-arts moves. Only now it's deadly serious and he can't afford to get it wrong. If it works, he'll choke Ron into unconsciousness. If it doesn't, he'll end up on the floor with the bigger man on top of him.

But it's the best chance he has.

Faking a right hook, Parker slips to his left, cutting an angle. Then he drags Ron's right arm across, moving until he's facing the other man's back. Parker jumps on Ron's shoulders like a monkey. His right arm snakes around the bigger man's neck as he winds his legs around his thighs.

Wearing Parker like a backpack, Ron staggers forward, bent in half. His hands pull at Parker's forearm, which is now wrapped around his throat. With his left forearm, Parker pushes the back of Ron's head forward and down, reinforcing the move with his chest. He doesn't know what he'll do if he gets thrown. He feels exhausted, his perch tenuous. He doesn't have any more energy to give, but he knows he can't stop. He wiggles his right arm to fit it more snugly across the carotids on the sides of the throat. His arms are crossed, with Ron's neck in the middle. With a grunt, Parker ratchets his elbows closer and closer together.

Finally Ron makes a rattling sound and falls to his knees. Parker doesn't let up the pressure. And then Ron falls facedown on the linoleum and doesn't even try to catch himself. Only then does Parker loosen his grip and unhook his legs.

Tugging his arm free, Parker gets to his feet. He kicks Ron in the side, but Ron doesn't move. He finally allows his focus to expand. That's when he sees Amina holding the fire extinguisher over one shoulder, ready to step in if Parker's plan failed.

"Thank you," he says. His heart is beating so hard, he can feel it in his ears and fingertips. He has to brace his hands on his knees, and suddenly he's worried that he might go tumbling to the floor next to Ron.

"Are you okay?" he asks.

Amina's eyes are huge. She manages a nod.

"Are you?"

ON THE TRIGGER

*C*HAOS, MIRANDA THINKS, HER HANDS slick on what was once Cole's rifle as they march past the newly opened gate and into the hall. That's the only word for what's happening. In her plan, she had imagined that everyone would be focused on her threat to kill Cole. Of course, her plan hadn't included all the suicide vests blowing up. Luckily, Cole's discarded vest had been far enough away that her group hadn't been hurt.

Seizing a chance to escape, some hostages are now running past Miranda, through the food court and into the mall. A guy with a shaved head who darts out of the Shoe Mill even has a handgun, but since he doesn't point it at Miranda as he runs past her, she decides she doesn't care. At the far end of the hall, other hostages are trying to crawl through the broken-out lower pane of one of the exit doors, which are still bike-locked together.

Miranda sticks to her plan. She has to make sure that their little crew plus Parker and Moxie get out of here safely. She ignores the smell of smoke, the sound of thundering water, and the sights of a murdered hostage and the pieces of the killer who died when his suicide vest exploded.

They go farther into the hall, Miranda marching Cole and his brothers ahead of her. But then Zach, the one code-named Zulu, the smaller of the two, runs toward a bench and snatches something from underneath it. When he straightens up and turns back, he's holding a rifle in his arms.

Miranda freezes. Where did it come from? It must have belonged to the dead killer. Everything slows down. With laser-like focus, Miranda watches Zulu's finger find the trigger. It feels as if she has all the time in the world to step to one side, to get out of the line of fire. She pictures it in great detail, how the bullet will sail harmlessly past her. Her thoughts feel sluggish, dreamlike.

But then with slowly dawning horror Miranda realizes that her body is actually doing nothing. It's not moving out of the way. She's not even pulling the trigger on her own rifle. She's like a spectator, watching as her own life comes to an end. Frozen.

With a smirk on his lips, the killer looks straight into Miranda's eyes through the holes in his mask. His own are icy blue, and there's a mole just underneath his left eyebrow.

Zulu's knuckle flexes as his finger tightens on the trigger.

All Miranda manages to do is suck in a breath. *This is it.*

But instead of the stutter of bullets, there's only a

click. Miranda blinks. Zulu squeezes the trigger again and again, which produces only more clicks. The rifle must have been damaged when its owner's vest exploded.

With an irritated grunt, Zulu grabs the rifle by the barrel, first with one fist, then the other. He hefts it over his shoulder like a bat, then steps forward as he swings it in a wide arc. His eyes are pinned on Miranda, but Grace is the person closest to him. With a horrible hollow sound, the stock strikes her temple. She stumbles sideways and goes down on one knee. Zulu hefts the rifle again.

"No!" Cole yells. "Don't hurt Grace!" Suddenly the scissors from Culpeppers's storeroom are in his hand. And then they're sticking out of his brother's neck, right where it meets his shoulder. Zulu drops the rifle, then stumbles backward. He sits heavily, his back against the Coach store's window, his eyes wide.

Grace grabs up the broken rifle and points it at him.

The killer pulls off his mask. Then his hands go to the handle of the scissors.

"Don't pull it out, Zach!" Cole yells, but his brother doesn't listen. And suddenly bright red blood is fountaining. A burst of noise at the entrance makes Miranda turn her head. On the far side of the glass doors is an army of uniforms. Some of the men and women have bolt cutters, some have pry bars, and all of them have guns. One by one the doors pop open and the cops surge in, shouting.

"EVERYBODY FREEZE!"

"DROP YOUR WEAPONS!"

"PUT YOUR HANDS ON TOP OF YOUR HEADS!"

Miranda drops her rifle, as does the guy with gauges

who had earlier taken the security guard's gun. Javier throws down his BB gun.

But Grace is still holding the jammed rifle, staring at Zulu and the blood spurting from his neck. And she doesn't move.

Miranda sees what the cops must. A woman with an assault rifle, seconds away from finishing off a gravely wounded hostage.

One of the cops trains his pistol on her. "Drop your weapon!" he roars. "Now!"

"Grace!" Miranda shouts, trying to break the spell. "Grace!"

But Grace doesn't move. She doesn't even blink.

Miranda watches the cop take careful aim. "Grace!" she screams again.

Just as Cole leaps in between Grace and the cop.

And the cop's bullet that was meant for Grace strikes Cole instead. He makes a terrible groan as he lands on the floor next to his brother.

Grace finally drops the rifle. She falls on her knees beside Cole. Screaming, screaming.

OVER

T'S OVER. AT THE COP'S COMMANDS, PARKER raises his hands, ignoring how the movement makes something grate in his side. Ignoring how his left pinky finger juts out at a weird angle from the rest of his hand.

The girl in the bloodstained shirt is screaming over the dead or wounded killers, Mole and Nicholas—the brother who stabbed him, the one Miranda marched in and who just got shot by the cops. Ron is still unconscious.

That leaves Wolf, and no one should leave Wolf.

Because instead of raising his hands, he bolts. As he runs, he reaches into the back of his waistband and pulls out something long and silver. It's that pistol with a silencer screwed onto the end, the one he used to shoot the guy whose phone rang. And then he darts toward Stanford and snatches Moxie out of her arms.

A cold fist of horror squeezes Parker's heart as Wolf points the gun at his sister's head.

"Parker!" Moxie screams, her arms reaching out to him. "Parker!"

ALL TOO MUCH

I T'S ALL TOO MUCH, MIRANDA THINKS AS SHE looks at Grace screaming over the bodies of Cole and his brother—only a few feet apart from each other. There's been so much carnage today. She can't do this anymore. She just can't. She squeezes her eyes closed.

But then above the shouts and screams of the hostages and the orders of the police, she hears a little voice shrieking.

She opens her eyes. Her stomach bottoms out. *No*, she thinks. *No, please, God, I'm not seeing this.*

Facing the police, one of the killers is holding Moxie tight against his chest with his left arm. His other hand has shoved the silenced pistol so tightly under her chin that it's forcing her small tearstained face to look up at the ceiling.

Moxie must know that it's a gun, because she's not squirming, not kicking her feet. Instead, she is perfectly still.

Miranda fights off a surge of nausea.

"Moxie! No! Moxie!" Parker's voice hitches and rises a notch. His empty hands reach out to her. He's about twenty feet away, but it's clear he doesn't dare go any closer.

The cops nearest the killer go still and watchful. Nothing moves but their eyes. The stillness ripples out as hostages and rescuers alike realize the horror is still not over.

"Back off or I'm going to kill this kid!" the killers' leader says. His voice cuts through the remaining din. "You need to get me a car. And then you're going to let me walk out of here."

No one moves. One of the policemen says in a slow and careful voice, "Okay, let's talk about this."

"Don't talk," he commands. "Do." He shifts the pistol so that it's pressed against Moxie's arm. "Get me that car. NOW. Or I'll start by shooting her in the hand or the foot."

If he leaves with Moxie, then she's dead. It's as simple as that. Discarded as soon as she's no longer needed. Or killed in a high-speed chase. Or when a policeman's bullet misses its intended target.

And if she dies, Miranda is sure that a big part of Parker will too.

Someone has to stop this.

Miranda remembers the scarves stuffed in her pocket, the ones they had originally planned to use to tie up anyone who came to check out the remote-control car. Now she pulls out a length of silky fabric and loops an end tight around each hand. The killer's attention is on the cops facing him. Not on the hostages behind him.

Before she can think better of it, Miranda runs up behind him, ignoring how the broken glass bites at her stockinged feet. She loops the scarf over his head and around his neck and then jerks back as hard and as fast as she can. He staggers back, falling to his butt, which sends Miranda to her knees. As his left hand rises to claw at the scarf, Moxie squirms free and runs to Parker. But the killer doesn't loosen his grip on the pistol. In fact, he keeps rotating his hand so that his gun is pointing behind him. Pointing right at her. Desperate to choke off his oxygen, Miranda pulls even harder. But she still sees his finger begin to tighten on the trigger.

With a flat clang, scorching metal punches her forehead, snapping it back. Hot blood pours down her face.

Then everything goes white.

MURDERS, HOSTAGE TAKING AT PORTLAND'S FAIRGATE MALL REVEALED TO BE SMOKESCREEN FOR $22 MILLION HEIST

(Associated Press)

Portland, Ore.—The FBI has revealed that the brazen shooting spree and hostage taking at Portland's Fairgate Mall last December was not just an act of domestic terrorism but also a distraction that allowed thieves to make off unmolested with more than $22 million in precious metals. The thieves are still at large, and the gold and silver they stole has not yet been recovered.

Nineteen people died in the attack, including three of the killers. Another twenty-three people were wounded. Several victims are still undergoing treatment for their injuries.

The group behind the attack, Liberty Makers, have in the past described themselves as patriots. They claim that the greatest threat America faces is not from hostile countries or Islamic terrorists but from the federal government. Authorities say group members are heavily armed extremists with an anti-government mindset. Many are current or former members of the military.

Mark Goforth of the Southern Poverty Law Center says, "The core ideas of these so-called patriot groups relate to the fear that elites in this country and around the world are nefariously moving us toward a one-world government."

The group was led by a charismatic ex-Marine named Karl McKinley. Other members included the three Bond brothers. Gabriel and Zach Bond had both been honorably discharged from the army after serving in Iraq and Afghanistan. Their younger brother, Nicholas "Cole" Bond, had recently graduated from high school. All three had trouble finding jobs that paid much more than minimum wage. Disillusioned, they joined Liberty Makers. The two older brothers had finally gotten work as security guards at Fairgate Mall. There, they introduced another security guard, Ron Skinner, to their cause. Tim Hollingsworth, a sixth Liberty Maker who joined the assault at the mall, had a long criminal record for petty crimes such as shoplifting and public drunkenness. Hollingsworth, along with Nicholas and Zach Bond, ultimately died in the mall.

What the others in the group didn't know was that McKinley had become disillusioned. Even though he had founded the group, he no longer believed it was possible to change society. So he decided to use Liberty Makers for his own purposes. He had learned about a shipment of gold and silver bars that would be aboard a tractor-trailer traveling from Boise, Idaho, to a processing plant in Vancouver, Washington. He wanted to rob the truck but needed a distraction so that he could get away clean.

The attack at Fairgate Mall provided that distraction. He persuaded the group that a blitz attack on the mall, followed by the holding of hostages, would bring needed attention to their cause.

McKinley's plan worked. By the time the theft of the precious metals was reported, all law enforcement within a hundred miles was busy responding to the unfolding tragedy at Fairgate Mall. A robbery, even one of such high-value items, had to be put on the back burner.

In the intervening weeks, authorities have not been able to locate McKinley or any associates he may have had and they fear that he may have fled the country. The two surviving attackers—Skinner and Gabriel Bond—claim to have had no knowledge of McKinley's secondary plan and not to know his current whereabouts.

TOGETHER, WE CAN MAKE A DIFFERENCE

3:53 P.M.

FIVE MONTHS LATER

CARRYING THE CARDBOARD TRAY FROM Perk Me Up, Miranda takes a deep breath and steps into the food court. Fairgate Mall looks like it did just before the shooting started five months ago. Then as now, people are eating, chatting, checking their phones, carrying shopping bags, bustling in and out of stores. The Christmas music has been replaced with something more generic. In a flash of memory, Miranda sees that bell ringer again, with the slogan on her red bucket. "Together, we can make a difference."

In her mind's eye, she can also still see the bodies, the blood, the broken glass and overturned chairs. See Gabriel Bond gliding down the escalator, unhurriedly raising his automatic rifle to shoot the wounded woman lying at its foot. Smell the smoke, the fire extinguisher's chemicals, and the stench of her own fear. Hear the gunshots, the fire alarm, the screams, the explosions.

This is the first time Miranda has been back since the night the paramedics carried her out. Now it takes all her willpower to keep moving toward the table where Javier, Amina, Parker, and Grace are waiting.

The five of them have stayed in loose touch, mostly by text. This is only the second time they've all been together since that terrible day. The first was a few days into the new year, when they were honored by the mayor for bringing an end to what is now called the Siege of Fairgate. Miranda thinks it sounds medieval, like what happened here involved castle walls and boiling oil and heads on spikes. Maybe it did. Just more modern versions of those things.

To a chorus of thank-yous from the others, she sets the tray down next to two red roses, each wrapped in green florist's paper, that are sitting in front of Grace.

Javier reaches for his plain black coffee, while Amina finds her peppermint tea. Grace picks up her coffee. Parker, like Miranda, ordered a latte. Lifting it in her direction, he gives her a smile.

Even though Parker is the one Miranda talks to the most, she doesn't know how to categorize their relationship. Being with him reminds her of the worst and best parts of herself. Of how far she has come from that afternoon in his basement. But there are times she doesn't want to be reminded of who she used to be. Of what she went through.

"It's like it never happened," Miranda says as she looks around the space.

"There's not even a plaque." Amina unclips her Culpeppers name tag.

Parker shrugs. "It's not like they could just tear down the mall and start from scratch." It's an old discussion between him and Miranda, one that began in the hospital after her dad told her the mall was already planning on reopening.

All of them had spent the night on the same ward. Grace had a concussion. Javier underwent surgery to clean up his wounds and stitch them closed. Parker's nose and finger and two of his ribs had been broken when the other hostages were forced to beat him, and he had cracked his tailbone when he slipped and fell. Even Amina had been hospitalized as a precaution.

Although Miranda had been sure that she was either blind or dying—or both—it turned out that Gabriel Bond's bullet had only grazed her scalp. An inch lower, and the bullet would have directly hit her brain, which was what she thought had happened. Blood had filled her eyes, leaving her temporarily blinded.

In the ambulance, she kept asking the crew if she was going to die. They said no, but it seemed liked the kind of faux reassurance you would offer someone who *was* dying.

But it turned out to be the truth. After she was cleaned up, Miranda could see again. Before stitching the wound closed, the doctor had shaved a spot on the top of her head bare, leaving what looked like a two-inch-wide part. Five months later, it's filled in with short hair.

Now Miranda shakes her head, trying to clear away the thoughts. She turns to Grace. "I like your new 'do."

Grace's hair is a bright-blue bob. It's so obviously a wig that it looks like a happy choice. And maybe it is.

"I figure why hide it?" She smiles. "And I've always wanted blue hair." Grace looks healthier than when they were all trapped in the storeroom together. Her face is fuller and there's color in her cheeks. "They say that, after chemo, your hair can come back completely different, like another color, or supercurly if it used to be straight or vice versa. I figure that after blue hair, it won't feel as big a change if something happens." She takes a deep breath. "Can you guys excuse me for a second?"

Picking up the two roses, she pushes back her chair. The others watch in silence as she walks toward the hall where the hostages were penned up. Bending down, she lays one rose on the floor, at the spot where Cole took a bullet for her. A few people watch her curiously, but most don't even notice her amid the bustle. Then she walks back to the food court, to the place where her mom's body had lain. This time Grace goes down on one knee and closes her eyes for a long moment.

When she returns, Javier says, "I'm sorry to say this, Grace, but someone's just gonna pick those up and throw them away. Probably the guy they hired to replace me. Management doesn't like there to be any reminders of what happened here."

Before they reopened the food court and the hall, the mall's owners held an interfaith ceremony featuring everything from a Catholic priest to a local shaman. Prayers were offered, sage burned. And then the shopping resumed.

Right after the shooting, the mall had fired Javier, claiming that they had had no idea that he was undocumented. After an outcry on social media—started by Parker—he had been rehired, in an even better position.

Grace makes a face. "They can pretend it never happened, but I can't. None of us can. What happened that day is always going to be a part of us." Her eyes grow wet. "At least I'm still alive to remember. At first I wondered why my mom had to die when I was the one who was already sick. I'm still seeing a counselor to deal with both of those things, and she's helped me mostly get past that guilt. And of course I've got my dad and my sister and my friends to talk to. But they don't understand what it was like the way you guys do. Cole killed my mom—and then he saved me. I'm still trying to figure out how the same person could have done both."

"He would have hated being locked up in prison," Miranda says. "Maybe he saw dying as the better choice."

"Do you think Cole really knew that was going to happen?" Parker looks doubtful.

Amina reaches out and takes Grace's hand. "I saw his face when he did it. He was trying to save you. I don't know if he knew he would die because of it, but that doesn't change what he did."

"He's still the kind of guy who thought it was okay to kill people," Parker says.

It's easy for Parker to see Cole in black and white,

Miranda thinks. He was never in the room with the five of them. He never heard Cole talk about the events that shaped his life and attitudes. Was Cole just a product of his circumstances? But that would negate both the bad things and good things he had done.

"Cole was racist," Javier says. "*And* he saved me from bleeding to death. Both things are true."

The five of them sit in silence with this for a minute.

Finally Miranda leans toward Javier. "How's the new job going?"

He runs his fingers through his black hair. "They call what I do maintenance engineer, but it's really running the heating and cooling systems. But now I'm thinking about going to college to be a real engineer. Amina's dad"—Amina and Javier exchange a smile—"helped me find an immigration lawyer. She's working pro bono. That means for no money. She says I can get a special visa when I testify about the killers, one that'll make me legal."

Amina asks, "How about your sister, Parker? How's Moxie doing?"

Parker digs his phone out of his pocket and passes it around so they can see Moxie's picture. In it, she's grinning and pointing at a missing front tooth.

A shadow crosses Grace's face as she says, "She's adorable." Miranda wonders if Grace is thinking that her treatment might leave her sterile. "Does she ever talk about what happened?"

Parker shrugs. "My parents made both of us go to therapy, but for Moxie it seems like most of it just rolled off." Miranda knows the same has not been true for him.

"My dad wants me to tell my story for my college essays." He blows air through pursed lips as he looks down at his hands, which are clenched into fists. "But that just seems wrong."

"Everyone always asks about it anyway," Amina says. "Might as well put it to some use." She touches her headscarf. "People are always staring at me, and not just in Culpeppers. Half of them ask if I'm the one they read about. The other half still call me a terrorist or tell me to go back to my country. Like you can't be both Muslim and American."

"They forget that the guys who did this were born here." Javier's mouth twists.

Miranda finds herself saying what she's been thinking for a few months. "Sometimes I think that they weren't really completely wrong about everything." She waves her hand at the throngs of shoppers. "It can't all be about buying stuff. Our priorities *are* sort of wrong."

"Their priorities weren't any better. Conspiracy theories." Grace shifts uncomfortably, as if remembering how she agreed with Cole about some things. "Killing people to make their point. Or that McKinley guy, pretending that he had a cause, when really all he wanted was millions in gold."

Karl McKinley, the one the others called Kilo, is still at large. Miranda figures with that much gold you could buy the best fake ID in the world. Buy yourself plastic surgery to make your face match your new papers.

"What do you think our priorities should be, then?" Javier asks.

"Maybe this sounds corny," Miranda says slowly, "but I think it all comes down to love. Loving people. Doing what you love." Miranda started a Narcotics Anonymous group at school and is thinking about being a counselor when she's older. Maybe she can help people figure out how to fill the hole inside them without stuffing it with pills or food or alcohol.

A woman in a pink turtleneck stands up from a table of other middle-aged women and ventures over to their table. "You're those kids, aren't you? The ones who took this place back from the killers." Her gaze is avid. Miranda feels her stomach curdle.

With each passing day, the public story gets simpler. Cole was never their friend. And the other hostages, even the one Parker nicknamed Heels, never fought back. Leaving only a band of plucky teens to save the day.

It's Miranda who finally nods. She's relieved when the other woman just says solemnly, "Thank you," before leaving. Then she tries to ignore how the other four women at the table openly stare, nudge each other, whisper, and snap pictures with their phones.

"So what about you, Miranda?" Grace asks. "How are you doing?"

She thinks a bit before answering. She sees her dad more often than she did before. Her mom has a tendency to hug her too tight and to want to talk about things, which Miranda has sort of grown to like. Her grades have gotten better. And she hasn't seen or talked to Matthew since the night it all happened.

"Still off Oxy, if you're wondering about that. It hasn't

been easy." She had admitted her addiction to them when she was in the hospital, when she refused to let the doctors give her anything, not even Advil. "But I went through the worst of the withdrawal here in the mall, when we were together."

"We wouldn't have made it, if it weren't for each other." Grace puts her cool hand on top of Miranda's. "We were meant to be together that day."

And then Javier, Amina, and Parker add their hands, until it's a stack of hands five high.

A NOTE FROM THE AUTHOR

Run, Hide, Fight Back is about something people fear a lot: a shooter in a public space and/or a terrorist attack (in this case, it's both). Who hasn't imagined what they would do if they were confronted by such a situation? There actually are things that we could do if we ever found ourselves in such a situation. In fact, the title was inspired by a Texas Homeland Security video called *Run, Hide, Fight* that gives practical tips on how to react.

Thirty-five years ago, my father, who was a county commissioner in Oregon, received death threats from a far-right group called Posse Comitatus. That sparked my interest in anti-government domestic terrorists like The Order, Timothy McVeigh, and the fictional villains in this book. Some federal and local law enforcement groups view the threat from these homegrown groups as at least equal to the threat from ISIS and other foreign Islamic terror groups.

Bill Krieg, a patrol lieutenant at the Appleton Police Department in Wisconsin and a defensive tactics instructor at Fox Valley Technical College, helped me when I was brainstorming the initial idea for this book—and even showed me how to use a Halligan tool. We met at the Writers Police Academy, run by veteran police investigator Lee Lofland. Multnomah County Sheriff's Office Search and Rescue volunteer Jake Keller was, as always, a great source of information. Robin Burcell, a former cop and an author in her own right, answered many "what if" questions. And Joe Collins, a paramedic and firefighter who has trained for various scenarios, including an attack on a shopping mall, gave me several devious ideas. Joe also answered my questions about guns and gave me ideas on how to treat a gunshot wound without a first aid kit. And I took a fascinating class on dealing with an active shooter from Mike Morton, a security specialist and former SWAT team member.

Elizabeth Bunga, a plans examiner for the City of Lake Oswego, helped me understand the rules for the required number of exits for stores in a shopping mall. Mark Berger, the president and chief product officer of Securitech Group, Inc., helped me figure out how to unlock doors that should be locked and lock doors that shouldn't be. Krys Jeffrey, executive team leader for assets protection at Portland's Galleria Target, explained the secret world of shoplifters. Professor Chris Bauer, a black belt in Brazilian jiujitsu who has made my own game so much better, helped me come up with the wrestling moves used in the climactic scene.

Even I find it hard to believe, but this is my twenty-fourth book with my agent, Wendy Schmalz.

My editor, Christy Ottaviano, pushed to make this book the best it could be. Jessica Anderson knows where all the bodies are buried. April Ward designs my amazing covers. Amanda Mustafic not only has the coolest bangs but can coordinate events across a half-dozen states. Other wonderful folks at Henry Holt include Lucy Del Priore, Melissa Croce, Katie Halata, Lara Stelmaszyk, Jennifer Healey, Molly Ellis, Lauren Festa, Morgan Rath, Allison Verost, and Mark Von Bargen.

9/19